Shaloha Gems

TERRY CHODOSH

*Helping talented writers
publish exceptional books.*

This is a work of fiction. References to real people, events, establishments, organizations, or locales are intended only to provide a sense of authenticity and are used fictitiously. All other characters, and all incidents and dialogue are drawn from the author's imagination and are not to be construed as real.

This book is dedicated to my long-suffering wife Nancy, who puts up with a kitchigai (crazy) husband, and her mother's family in Okinawa who suffered greatly in the battle of Okinawa. Also to the members of the 100th Infantry Battalion and the 442nd Regional Combat Team made up of Japanese American soldiers, which was the most decorated unit in the US military during the Second World War. Amongst them was my wife's uncle, Charlie Arakaki. The 100th Infantry Battalion was part of the 5th Army, in which my father, Master Sergeant Zelman Chodosh, was a soldier.

This book is also dedicated to the brave members of the Israel Defense Forces, who are fighting to ensure that concentration camps like Dachau never exist again.

CHAPTER 1
GOLDY'S DIAMONDS
AREN'T FOREVER

Abe Goldstein stared out of the barred back-office window of his company, Goldy's Diamonds & Gems, which overlooked the rainy and grey 47th Street Diamond District. The grimy man-trap door, the hallway entrance, and the lone off-duty NYPD officer outside told the story of a city that had seen its best days and was going downhill faster than a Coney Island roller coaster.

Abe thought even a roller coaster goes back up again, but there was no way in hell that New York would make a comeback. Since the Covid lockdowns, the huge spike in crime, and the exit of most of his retail client base out of New York City to South Florida, his retail business had dropped off a cliff, and his wholesale business was barely keeping him afloat.

Today, Abe was meeting with his longtime friend and accountant Adam Bushkin, whom Abe jokingly referred to as "Bombastic Buskin," like Johnny Carson's accountant who had once recommended that Carson invest in X-rated bookstores in Iran.

Like Abe, Adam was an Orthodox Jew who kept kosher, observed Shabbat, and wore the yarmulke to show reverence for Hashem (God). He looked and acted like a pudgy version of the old-time comedian Red Buttons, wearing the mischievous look of a man always on the verge of laughter. This was their quarterly meeting before tax filing, and Abe looked forward to it like he did a root canal.

"So, Bombastic," he said, "give me the good news first so I can smile for five seconds at least."

Adam reported that, "The good news is that Katz's Deli on Houston Street downtown has a new lunch special: all-you-can-eat kosher pickles with your fifty-dollar pastrami sandwich. The bad news is that revenues have sunk into the toilet by over 50 percent. I hate to tell you, Abe, but your business is on life support. You can't hold on much longer. I suggest you consider selling and moving out-of-state. My other clients in the diamond business have moved to Florida — Miami, Boca Raton, and Palm Beach. The business district in those cities looks like Tel Aviv."

Abe chewed his lower lip unhappily. "My diamond clients who moved there tell me the competition is so fierce that they're all undercutting each other, and their margins are slimmer than the Jewish book of business ethics. They are making bupkis down there."

Abe's father, Moishe, had founded the business in New York City after the war. Moishe was a Holocaust survivor of the Dachau concentration camp and still had the tattoo on his left forearm. Now he had a scraggly white beard and hunched back from old age, and the demeanor of a man who had seen much suffering in his life.

Before the war, Moishe's family had established diamond businesses in Amsterdam and Antwerp. They'd lost everything after the Germans conquered the Netherlands. Moishe's parents, brothers, and sisters all perished in the camps. Moishe was the youngest and survived to be liberated by the United States Army. Later, he was sent to a displaced persons' camp and was adopted by the Goldstein's, distant relatives who were also in the diamond business in New York.

Abe resembled his father as a young man, but even more so the movie star Adam Sandler, with curly brown hair, a prominent nose, and a cleft chin that accentuated his square jawline.

"Bombastic," he exclaimed, "what am I going to do? We still have a great supply line of diamond cutters in Tel Aviv and connections with De Beers in Johannesburg. Come up with something!"

A week later, Adam called Abe and set up a lunch meeting at Katz's. The men slid into their usual booth, gripping pastrami sandwiches thick enough to choke a horse. They munched on the endless pickle barrel gracing each table.

"There's enough salt in these pickles to kill the entire cardiology wing at Bellevue Hospital," Abe joked.

"Abe, you are a young man, only forty. It will take at least fifty years for Katz's pickles to kill you — unless you marry a Jewish yenta. Then I give you about twenty years or less."

Abe wiped his mouth on a napkin and shot Adam a dour look. "Don't mention marriage. My mother is driving me crazy. She even bought me an online subscription to JDate, that Jewish singles dating app. She put my photo and cell phone numbers on the site. I got meshuga women contacting me day and night. They only show headshots and describe themselves as voluptuous, so I am guessing that some of these women are big enough to put license plates on them."

His accountant smiled. "Abe, don't choke on your pastrami sandwich when I tell you this, but I think I found a gem of a wedding/engagement ring company where the markups on diamond rings are double what they are in New York."

Abe arched a brow. "Oh, yes? Pray tell me where this gem is located."

"It's in Honolulu, Hawaii." Adam leaned across the table, eyes twinkling. "This company's revenues have dropped off a cliff because the Japanese tourist industry died due to the Covid restrictions on Japanese returning to Japan. They're required to go into quarantine prison for two weeks, so the owner of this company called Aloha Gems, Chikara Arakaki, wants to retire and sell his business."

Adam shrugged. "When the Japanese tourists return to the islands in droves, this company will explode due to the huge multimillion-dollar Japanese wedding industry in Hawaii. It's big face for the Japanese to get married in Hawaii. They buy the rings there since diamond rings are twice as expensive in Japan. They set them up with wedding packages, including the rings, the hotels, the limousines, and the photographers."

Abe grunted; his interest piqued. "Go on."

Adam took a bite of his pastrami sandwich, gesturing with a pickle for emphasis. "The business has a relation-ship with Japan Airlines and the tour companies to funnel these wedding couples to Aloha Gems. If done right, the place is a gold mine. Since we have a great pipeline for rocks, no one there can undercut us on the cost of cut diamonds. We'll kill them, Abe! If the Honolulu company is successful, we can expand to Maui and the Big Island, maybe even to Guam."

Abe gave his friend a level stare. "Adam, the closest I've gotten to Japan was a dinner at Benihana steakhouse. Let me think about this."

As they pair left Katz's, they stepped over a homeless man lying outside the door and watched a mugger grab a woman's purse and run down the street.

"Adam, is there at least a kosher restaurant in Honolulu?"

"Yep, the Shalom Café in the same building as the Chabad House."

Abe nodded briskly. "Go ahead and book the flight."

They got a direct flight from JFK airport to Honolulu, which takes thirteen hours in the air. The time difference was six hours earlier, so they were exhausted upon arrival but were met near baggage claim by an Asian limousine driver holding a placard up with the name Goldstein. Next to the limo driver stood a beautiful Asian woman with long black hair and a porcelain complexion wearing a full-length muumuu, the traditional Hawaiian dress. When Abe and Adam identified themselves, the woman hung flower leis on each of them.

Kiyoko Arakaki was the daughter of the owner of Aloha Gems, Chikara Arakaki. She explained that the usual routine was to kiss their cheeks after she put the lei around their necks, but airport regulations required everyone to always wear a mask. Abe bashfully replied that since he was an unmarried Orthodox Jewish male, he was not supposed to touch an unmarried female who was not a relative.

After she turned away, Abe looked at Adam and whispered, "I like this place already."

Kiyoko brought Abe and Adam to their limo and directed the driver to take them to the Royal Hawaiian Hotel in Waikiki. She promised to meet them in the hotel lobby at 9:00 a.m. the next morning and walk them to her family's shop nearby in the Royal Hawaiian shopping center.

The next morning, Adam and Abe were having coffee at the hotel restaurant on the water. A slight trade wind was blowing. They watched the gentle waves lap the shore as surfers lazily paddled out to the shore break. Soft Hawaiian music played in the background, with flowers artistically placed on their table setting. Abe sipped his smooth as silk 100-percent Kona coffee.

"Are you sure the coffee is kosher?" he asked.

"I checked with the rabbi on this," Adam said. "Coffee is inherently kosher unless they use pig dreck as fertilizer."

Abe replied, "You are joking, of course, but I ask you, why didn't we make this move years ago?"

Adam gave one of his signature shrugs. "Covid set the stage for companies in Hawaii with high overhead to go out of business. A high percentage of their service industry workers had to work two to three jobs to make ends meet. When Covid hit, there were layoffs, and many service workers left for the mainland, primarily to Las Vegas, which the Hawaiians call the Ninth Island. The revenues of companies like Aloha Gems were decimated by the lack of Japanese tourism and the exit of many local middle-class Hawaiian residents."

He sipped his coffee. "With our pipeline of cut gems directly from our own diamond cutters in Tel Aviv and the pipeline of stones from South Africa, we can undercut any diamond business in the Pacific. We'll bring in our own back-office staff and a few salespeople, but most of the personnel will have to be retained from Chikara's staff. We must set up a consulting and non-compete agreement with them, or this won't work."

Abe nodded agreement. "Makes sense."

"Of course, the purchase price must also be right," Adam continued. "I'm guessing he'll hit us with the pre-Covid valuation of the company, but I am not going for that. Give me time to crunch the numbers with their office manager and accountant and look at their tax returns. And by the way, I got a great name for the company: Shaloha Gems." He waved his hands, mushing the two words together. "Shalom and Aloha. It's a natural."

Kiyoko met Abe and Adam in the hotel lobby precisely at 9:00 a.m. and walked with them to her father's store. The Royal Hawaiian shopping center catered to a high-end clientele, as evidenced by the presence of designer bag and luxury watch shops, where Japanese, Korean, and increasingly Chinese buyers rushed to make purchases. Adam mentioned to Abe that many Asian people, especially Chinese, purchase luxury watches and jewelry to move money across international borders and then resell the watches and jewelry.

Kiyoko explained that her father had their entire staff at the location to greet them as a show of big face to a potential owner. As they entered the store, Abe and Adam noticed the signs were in English, Chinese characters, and written Japanese, which is Hiragana and Katakana, foreign words morphed into Japanese.

The entire staff bowed as the trio entered the store. The owner, Chikara Arakaki, was a stout seventy-year-old Okinawan man with bushy eyebrows. He and his son Kazuo greeted them with handshakes and small gifts. Chikara was dressed in a jacket and tie, as was his son, which was very unusual for Hawaii. Chikara told them they were honored to have the two men visit their store and that his son Kazuo was the office manager and book-keeper for the business. Abe introduced Adam as his accountant and bookkeeper and suggested that at one point, he and Kazuo could crunch some numbers.

Chikara invited Abe and Adam into his private office to have tea and chat about the possible purchase of his family business. Chikara described the company's history from its beginnings when his father Masaru Arakaki came home from serving in the United States Army in Europe during World War Two. After the war, Masaru studied gemology under a kind Jewish diamond merchant, and started the family business with his guidance and support.

The company struggled for many years until the Japanese economic invasion in the 1980s, when the Japanese made purchases of luxury residences at exorbi-tant prices (since, at that time, the yen was strong against the US dollar). It was big face for a Japanese person to own luxury Hawaiian real estate. Along with that came entirely new industries, including the Japanese wedding industry. The Japanese real estate market in Hawaii crashed due to the Japanese economy going into the toilet, but the wedding industry remained.

It was cheaper, Chikara explained, for the Japanese to get married in Hawaii than in Japan since every relative had to be invited, and gifts had to be sent to all the invi-tees. Enormous stress and expense ensued. So, a gigantic wedding industry developed in Hawaii from Japan. Hotels and tour operators were involved, as well as limo services, wedding photographers, flower stores, and wedding dress companies.

And, of course, engagement and wedding rings were

needed since the cost of diamonds in Japan was double that in the United States. Here in Hawaii, there was a *keiretsu* network of companies (mostly Japanese-owned) that worked together for mutual benefit and to control the lucrative wedding industry.

"As you may know," Chikara said, "Covid has tremendously damaged that industry, and since many of our best people have retired or left the islands, I've decided to sell my business and retire to my coffee farm on the Big Island." He glanced at Kazuo with mild regret. "My son is not interested in taking over the business. But my daughter, Kiyoko, whom you already met, is a certified gemologist interested in staying in the business."

Chikara regarded the two men impassively. "To be frank, my company has a stellar reputation for honesty and integrity in the community. We look seriously at giving back to the local people in various ways, including supporting charitable events like the local Japanese community's cherry blossom festival. It is a weeklong event, and at the conclusion, a beauty contest comprised of young Japanese and Okinawan women is held to select the cherry blossom queen." He allowed himself a proud smile. "I have to brag that my daughter Kiyoko has won the contest before. We are of Okinawan descent, a separate but similar culture to the Japanese. We hope that if you purchase our company, your company will maintain that level of community support."

Abe met his gaze and gave a respectful nod.

"All of our staff speak Japanese," Chikara continued, "which is an essential element of doing business with our customers, especially the Japanese tourists. I have done some due diligence on your financial situation, reputation, and integrity through my contacts in the New York diamond industry. To your credit, they give your family high marks in an industry where that is a rarity."

Abe and Adam shared a quick look. *So far, so good,* Abe thought. *But does he know that Goldy's Diamonds & Gems is sliding off a financial cliff—*

"I noticed that your retail business has dropped significantly," Chikara said, as Abe suppressed a grimace, "which is understandable where you are located. However, doing business in Hawaii is vastly different from doing business in New York. I can assure you my daughter can assist you in that area if this sale moves forward. I also must advise you that there is another possible purchaser of my business, a local Japanese competitor that I have had problems within the past. He has a poor reputation and is rumored to have some underworld connections. I am reluctant to sell to a person of that character. My son Kazuo oversees the money and the negotiations, but I will have the final say on that. Your man, Adam, and my son can sit down for a few hours today and tomorrow morning to go over the books in detail, and we shall see what happens."

That evening, Abe and Adam had dinner at the only certified kosher restaurant in Honolulu, the Shalom Café on Kapiolani Boulevard in the same building as the Chabad house, an Orthodox Jewish congregation. As they sat down, the rabbi dropped by the table to introduce himself. Rabbi Shmuley was a man in his forties with a curly red beard and an Australian accent.

After introductions, Rabbi Shmuley said, "I heard that you were visiting from New York and were looking to buy a business here."

Abe replied, "Rabbi, you heard right. I hear there are a

lot of Israelis in the jewelry business, as well as the skin-care cosmetic business in Honolulu."

The rabbi told them that that was true and that if Abe would like, he could introduce them to some people in that industry in the Islands. Shmuley added that his son Mendel ran a kosher food distribution company and that they would have no problem obtaining kosher food in Honolulu.

After the rabbi left, Adam turned his old friend. "You know, Abe, a few of my contacts warned me that some of the Israelis in Honolulu are less than reputable. "

Abe flipped through the menu. "Bombastic, that's why I pay you the big bucks to clue me in on stuff like this. What's your take on the revenue and organization of Chikara's business?"

"I studied the books with Kazuo, and from what I can tell, predictably, the company's revenues were outstanding in 2018 and 2019, but dropped off in 2020 and 2021 due to the drop in Japanese tourism due to Covid. As expected, they want to value the company based on their 2018 and 2019 revenues. I suggested averaging out the revenues over the last four years and producing an average valua-tion, but they pushed back on that."

Adam sipped his water. "I think that Chikara wants his former employees to be retained and properly taken care of. This guy is a real mensch, and I think that a commit-ment for us to hire at least some of his key employees will be an essential element in his decision. Think about it: if the other prospective purchaser came in, he wouldn't hire most of the employees, and the others would probably quit."

Abe smiled, grateful for the sound advice he always got from his longtime friend. Things were looking brighter after all. He squinted at the tropical sun slanting through the restaurant blinds. *Literally.*

"So, let's discuss this further with a strong one-to-two-year consulting and non-compete agreement," Adam said, signaling to the waiter. "I think the best way to get a feel for the company and how to handle these negotiations is to get to know Kiyoko and pick her brain about whether this possible purchase is a good fit for us." He frowned slightly. "Interesting that the company got its start through another Jewish diamond merchant, eh?"

Adam nodded. "I caught that, too. I wonder what the whole story was?"

Masaru Arakaki's Tale

AFTER WORLD WAR TWO ENDED, Sergeant Masaru Arakaki's platoon joined the 522nd artillery battalion in occupation duties around Donau worth, Germany near the banks of the Danube River where the 522nd spent the next six months.

One of the 522nd's duties was to gather displaced persons into a central area and return them to their home countries. Sergeant Masa became friendly with some of the concentration camp survivors who spoke English, providing them with rations and cigarettes. They told him that they worked in German munition factories and sabotaged many of the German artillery rounds. Masa recalled that several German artillery rounds from their feared 88 cannons were duds, which saved many of the soldiers in his platoon from certain death when the rounds failed to explode.

Just before the war officially ended on May 8, 1945, the 522nd was among the US forces at Berchtesgaden, Germany where it was believed that Hitler would make his last stand. It was not meant to be. Hitler committed suicide on April 30, 1945.

On May 8, Sergeant Masa was going to the train station to join his unit when he read the headline in the Stars and Stripes that Germany had surrendered and the war in Europe was over.

In August 1946, Sergeant Masa, members of his platoon, and others from the 442nd RCT and the 522nd Artillery battalion boarded trains to France, and when they arrived in San Francisco the 442nd got on the Liberty ship SS Waterbury Victory that arrived in Honolulu on August 9, 1946.

Katsue Nishihama was waiting at the dock at Pearl Harbor for Sergeant Masa. She gave Masaru a red ilima flower lei with a traditional kiss, and they embraced at the dock. It seemed like they held their embrace forever. When Masaru excitedly asked, "Will you marry me? Aishitemasu (I love you). I want you to be my wife."

"Yes, yes, hai, hai," cried Katsue.

The members of the 442nd received a welcome home ceremony hosted by the governor at Iolani Palace and were discharged from the U.S. Army out of Fort Shafter on Oahu.

Katsue's parents invited Masaru to their home for dinner that Saturday evening after Masaru came home. It was the first time that he had ever been to their home, which was in a wealthier neighborhood in Manoa.

Masaru wore his dress uniform and campaign metals, including his Purple Heart and Bronze Star, looking like the handsome, proud soldier that he had become.

"Sergeant Arakaki, we welcome you to our home," Taka Nishihama and his wife Reiko said warmly.

"Sir, please call me Masa."

After being home for six months and seeing Katsue almost every night, on her birthday at her family's residence over dinner he announced, "Mr. Nishihama, I want to marry your daughter, and would like you and Reiko's blessing."

Taka Nishihama had grown fond of the handsome young man. "Of course, you can marry my daughter. I want your strong blood in my grandson's veins. But how are you going to support her, young man?"

Katsue jumped in. "I spoke to Mr. Silverberg about Masa and set up a meeting with him and Masa tomorrow afternoon. Mr. Silverberg is a kind Jewish man, and I think he will like and hire Masa."

Masaru was introduced by Katsue to Hyman Silverberg, her employer at Hawaii Gems. Masa wore his army uniform bearing his medals and cut a dashing figure.

"Mr. Silverberg, this is my fiancé Masaru. He just got out of the army and would like to learn about the gem business."

Hyman sat with Masaru in his cluttered office with a mezuzah affixed to the doorway. "So young man, Katsue tells me that you were in Europe fighting the Germans, is that true?"

"Yes, sir, it is."

"Did you see any Jewish people in Europe?"

"Yes, sir, I did." He was silent for a moment, his gaze haunted. "It's not something I like to talk about, but we liberated a prison camp where many Jews had been killed. It was a horrible scene. I have tried to erase that from my memory."

Hyman shook his head and put a handkerchief to his eyes as he listened to Masaru. "I'm sorry, I do apologize," he said, his voice unsteady. "I had relatives there in Eastern Europe that I'm sure have perished." Hyman gathered his composure, studying the young veteran. "I see the Bronze Star for valor on your chest, tell me did you kill any of those bastard Germans?"

Masa lifted his chin. "Yes, sir, I did."

"Well, Masaru, I can tell you are a mensch, which means a man of character. You can work as my apprentice and I will teach you everything I know." He smiled. "It's unusual for a Japanese to work in this business, but let's give it a try."

So began Masaru Arakaki's beginnings in the diamond and gem business, running errands and then learning how to grade diamonds. Hyman Silverberg treated Masaru like the son he'd never had. Masa was a quick study, honest and hardworking. Soon thereafter, Hyman attended Masaru and Katsue's wedding at the Hongwanji mission, a first for Hyman.

Hyman was the only haole (Caucasian) at the ceremony, looking out of place wearing a suit and tie and a yarmulke. He hugged the bride and groom after the ceremony, though he had previously advised them that he could not attend the reception at the Natsunoya tea house since the food was not kosher.

The Natsunoya tea house overlooked Pearl Harbor in Alewa Heights, Oahu, a historical location where spies from the Japanese consulate had counted the ships on battleship row before December 7.

Masaru worked for Hyman Silverberg for five years and was made a part owner with the understanding he would purchase the business upon Hyman's retirement.

Soon after, Katsue and Masaru had a baby boy they named "Chikara," which means strength in Japanese.

After ten years, when Hyman retired in his seventies, Masaru took over the business and changed the name to "Aloha Diamonds." Later when his son was in his twenties, they moved their shop to the upscale Royal Hawaiian Shopping Center in Waikiki. Chikara took over the business years later and sent his young daughter Kiyoko to the gemology institute in Los Angeles to become a certified gemologist.

CHAPTER 2
ALOHA HAWAII

The next morning, Adam and Abe met Chikara, his son Kazuo, and Kiyoko at the Aloha Gems store. Chikara suggested that Adam meet the backroom and sales staff, many of whom were middle-aged Japanese women who had been at the company for over twenty years. Adam broke off with Kazuo and retired to the back room. Chikara indicated that he thought Abe should speak to Kiyoko about the business culture in Hawaii. A young Japanese couple entered the store and started browsing the wedding rings. One of the middle-aged saleswomen was working with them.

Abe watched the transaction with a keen eye. The conversation was mainly in Japanese, with some broken English thrown in. Lots of bowing took place, with the saleswoman bowing noticeably lower than the customers and offering them her *meishi*, presenting the business card with two hands to show respect. Even though Abe couldn't understand what they said, he didn't notice any aggressive attempt to close the sale as he would have done in New York.

He brought this up with Kiyoko. She explained that "to sell to the Japanese requires a very different sales technique. The Japanese do not respond positively to aggressive sales pressure. They go by trust, the reputation of the owners and the dealership. They consider a hard sales pitch that gives a discount as an insult. The sales pitch that we make is that you are a revered client, we are giving you the same price as we would our family, and we hope that you will let others know of the great service and quality that you received at our company.

"When the sale is completed, we will also give them a small gift called *omiyage*. A large purchase might be a tea set, and smaller purchases might include a basket of Hawaiian coffee, honey, and Macadamia nuts. These small things are very important to a Japanese client."

Abe nodded slowly, eager to learn the ropes. It was a far cry from New York City.

"In dealing with the Chinese," Kiyoko added, "it's a totally different approach. They want to undercut the price and walk out of here thinking they got the best bargain imaginable. They will play off other prices and even bring in their own stones and ask us to do the settings for cheap prices." She gave a crooked grin that made his heart flutter. "Still, they are happiest if they think they screwed you. Pardon the language. We don't do a lot of Chinese business."

Abe was fascinated and perplexed by this vast difference in the sales culture. "To me, given what you said, it's obvious why your family's business has been successful. My question is, since I am an outsider buying your family business, would the same level of trust apply?"

Kiyoko considered his question for a moment. "The Japanese would see the same salespeople and the same level of respect. It might take a while for the word to get around. Also, our strategic partners, the tour companies, Japan Airlines, and the hotels would have to be assured that nothing would change and that the integrity, value, and service would remain the same." She glanced around at the sales staff. "A key element is that the same up-front personnel would be there."

Abe smiled, admiring her obvious intelligence and expertise. "As I see it, you are an essential element to making my purchase of your father's company work for us. If the purchase goes through, I would like your commitment to having you sign a consultation agreement with our company for at least eighteen months. Would you agree to that?"

Kiyoko met his gaze. "I would be happy to assist, but you would have to speak to my father first, and you must also retain other key employees."

Abe's spirits lifted. "Absolutely, Kiyoko, absolutely."

She looked pleased. "My father suggested I take you around Honolulu and show you some items of interest. First, shall we get something to eat?"

"Let's go to the Shalom Café," he suggested. "The kosher restaurant on Kapiolani Boulevard. You can see a little of my world."

They drove in Kiyoko's high-end Lexus to the kosher restaurant. As they sat down at a table, Kiyoko noticed the bearded Orthodox Jews wearing their yarmulkes or kippah skullcaps and commented on the fringes hanging out of their pants. Abe explained that the kippahs were meant to show reverence for Hashem, the Hebrew term for God.

"The strings are called tzitzits, which are reminders to Orthodox Jews that they should try to follow the 613 mitzvot as described in the Torah, the Jewish Bible, or Old Testament," he explained.

When the food was served, Abe said a short prayer in Hebrew prior to eating. Kiyoko told him that the Japanese say *Itadakimasu*, an expression of gratitude for receiving the food, usually accompanied by rubbing your chopsticks together to get the splinters off the balsawood sticks.

"Kiyoko, the Jews don't waste a second rubbing anything together before they eat," Abe said dryly. "Just don't get between a Jew and a buffet table because you will be steamrolled!"

Kiyoko laughed. "Your religion is very interesting. I would like to learn about your Bible, the Torah. I think it contains great wisdom."

Abe replied, "Yes, of course, I would be happy to. If my purchase of your family's company goes through, I will teach you. But at the same time, you must teach me Japanese customs and language. Is it a deal?"

"Hai, wakarimasu. Yes, I understand." She dug into the meal with delicate gusto. "If you purchase the company, what are your plans? Will you bring your wife and children out with you to live here?"

Abe heaved a theatrical sigh. "Kiyoko, I have no wife or children, much to my Jewish mother's distress. She has gone as far as signing me up for a Jewish singles dating app called J-Date without my knowledge, putting my Yeshiva University photo on it, my email and cellphone. I had to change my number since I was getting calls from meshuga women day and night."

Her brow creased in puzzlement. "Meshuga?"

Abe twirled a finger. "Meshuga means Crazy. My

mother is obsessed with marrying me off to a nice Jewish girl so she can have some grandchildren."

She covered a giggle. "Abe, meshuga is a funny word. The word for crazy in Japanese is *kichigai*."

He filed that tidbit away, then cleared his throat and aimed for a casual tone. "So, what about you, Kiyoko? I take it that you're single as well?"

"Yes, I am. I'm thirty-five years old, which is considered ancient for a single Japanese or Okinawan woman. If I lived in Japan, I would be considered an old maid. I was engaged to be married to what we call a Glenn Miyashiro-type dull Japanese male, which is how a local comedian described the typical Hawaiian Japanese man."

Abe propped his chin on his hand, grinning now. "Oh?"

She smiled back, ticking off the list with her fingers. "He lives at home until he's thirty, wears glasses, went to Iolani High School and UH Manoa, studied accounting, and wears reverse print blue aloha shirts. His biggest thrill is to go to Las Vegas once a year, to go to a station casino, and buy beef jerky from Trader Joes to take back to Hawaii. He was my father's best friend's son, and they did their best to set us up. He was in his father's big accounting firm here and lived in a mansion on Hawaii Loa Ridge."

Abe winced, trying unsuccessfully not to laugh.

"I just could not go through with it," Kiyoko said with a rueful shake of her head. "My parents were very embarrassed when I returned his three-carat engagement ring, which he had purchased through our company. Of course, my father took the ring back, and the breakup caused a permanent rift in his friendship."

"I went to Iolani school and attended UH Manoa,

where I got my degree in geology. I then studied at the Gemology Institute of America in Los Angeles to get my certification. My father was upset that my brother Yoshi was not interested in going into the business." Her face fell for a moment, then brightened again.

"I'm not all work, though. I enjoy water sports. If you move here, you must take up surfing or outrigger canoe paddling to enjoy the Hawaiian lifestyle. I belong to the Outrigger Canoe Club here and am a member of a women's team that competes in races during Regatta season. I will take you and Adam there on Sunday if you like."

"I would be a fish out of water trying to surf or paddle," Abe confessed, "but maybe I'll give it a try. This is a million miles from Manhattan and Williamsburg, Brooklyn, where I grew up, but something told me it was time for a change. The grey misery of living and working in Manhattan was aging me."

He leaned back in the booth. She had been frank with him. He decided to open up a little, too. "I saw myself becoming my father in thirty or forty years, with a grey beard, stooped over his desk with his loop monocle on, examining diamonds until he was almost blind. Even though he is a successful businessman, having built his business from scratch, he is not a happy person. His time in a concentration camp has affected his life profoundly. He doesn't seem to ever enjoy life. I dread living like that. Maybe that's why I am enamored by Hawaii's laid-back attitude and the outdoor, healthy ocean lifestyle."

Kiyoko gave an encouraging nod, one finger curling a lock of silky black hair.

"The only exercise I got in New York was running to the subway." Abe snorted. "Lately, it was more like running for my life, with homicides up 50 percent in the city. I didn't want to live like that, didn't want to die from some thug stabbing me to death for my wallet, or some nut pushing me onto the subway tracks, or more likely dropping dead at my desk at sixty from eating one too many heart attack pastrami sandwiches."

Kiyoko nodded sympathetically.

"Can I be honest with you?" Abe drew a deep breath. "The moment I got off the plane and saw you put the flower lei around my neck, I told myself that as strange as it might seem, I felt that I belonged here, as far away from my old life as possible. I know this place has its problems, and I am an outsider here, especially in a Japanese-dominated industry. I have no illusions about the challenges I will face if we do purchase your father's business, but I have a good feeling about it. It feels right. Does that make sense?"

Her dark eyes were kind. "Abe, yes, it does. There are problems here, of course, some of them financial, some of them political. Our main competitor, Ono Diamond Engagement and Wedding Rings, has tried to take away our business using underhanded methods like bribery and even coercion of our strategic partners like tour operators who hand out our fliers and bring tourists to our store. We treat everyone with respect and integrity.

"There is also a political aspect to doing business in Hawaii. My father donates to the Democratic Party for every one of his employees, so if there is a problem, he can call someone, and it will be taken care of. That's how we do business in Hawaii."

She paused for a moment, seeming to gather her courage. "If I can now be honest with you, my father and brother are concerned that your New York aggressiveness will not go over well with the locals and the Japanese visitors. We can also help with political connections. By the way, the lieutenant governor and a US senator in Hawaii are Jewish."

Abe said, "That's why I need you to mentor us and help us navigate this world. We have the best diamond cutters that work for us in Tel Aviv and a worldwide network of gems and diamonds that can make this business a big success."

The rabbi came to the table, said hello to Abe, and introduced himself to Kiyoko. The rabbi asked how they were doing and if Abe was enjoying his time in Hawaii.

"Yes, Rabbi, I am."

"Will you be here for Shabbat dinner this Friday?"

"I will. "

"Good. I will introduce you to another guy in the jewelry business. His name is Gilad, and he is an Israeli who wants to meet you. Maybe he can be a good contact for you here."

Abe forced a smile, keeping his voice light. "Rabbi, I haven't even bought a company here yet. You are putting the cart before the horse."

"Maybe I am, but it will be great to have you here."

As they left the restaurant, Kiyoko mentioned that the rabbi was very nice and seemed enthused about him coming here.

"Kiyoko, the rabbi is a nice guy," Abe replied wearily, "but he is more enthused about having another wealthy benefactor to support his congregation. That's the way the Jews look at things."

Back at Aloha Gems, Abe and Kiyoko met up with Adam and her father and brother Kazuo, and they all sat down in the back office.

"We reached an impasse on the price of the business," Adam told Abe regretfully. "We are a few hundred thousand apart in the purchase price."

Abe replied, "Let's step back on this for a few days and give some thought to how this can work."

The two men attended Shabbat services and then went downstairs for dinner. As they were eating, the rabbi brought over two Israelis, one a man in his fifties named Gilad and another younger man in his late twenties named Yitzie.

Gil was portly and wore a heavy gold chain and gold president Rolex watch. Yitzie was another gold chain guy with an array of tattoos and earrings.

"Shabbat shalom, welcome to Hawaii," Gil said. They inserted some Hebrew into the conversation to check Abe and Adam's fluency. "Rabbi tells me you are from 47th Street in Manhattan. I know some people back there. Morty Glickman, a wholesaler for one. Knew him in the IDF. Good man."

"I know Morty," Abe replied. "He is also connected to the Israeli consulate there. What kind of jewelry business do you have, Gil?"

"I have a booth at the international marketplace in Waikiki and a storefront in Kona. I sell Hawaiian junk jewelry to tourists. I also have kiosks at the shopping centers here where I have kids selling skincare products. Yitzie here oversees the kiosks."

"Abe, can I give you some advice?" Yitzie asked. "In the high-end diamond business, you've got to compete against the Japanese-owned businesses fleecing the tourists from Japan, and that's going to be tough. I know some people here that might be able to give you some help. You know in case the locals give you a hard time."

Abe feigned innocence. "What kind of help are you talking about, Gil?"

"You are from New York." He lowered his voice a fraction. "I don't have to tell you what I mean."

Abe gave him a tight smile. "Nice meeting you. I've got to discuss some business with my partner here. Shabbat shalom."

"Okay, listen, we would like you to come over to my condo in Waikiki sometime for dinner. Glatt kosher, of course." Gil left his business card on the table.

"Sure, nice to meet you."

Adam turned to Abe. "I read these guys as two Moroccan Israeli hustlers. The last time I saw a gold chain that heavy, Mr. T was wearing it in the *Rocky* movie. What I can't figure out is how he knew we were from 47th Street and in the high-end diamond business. We never mentioned that to the rabbi. He also mentioned Morty Glickman who moves rocks but also works in the security section of the consulate."

A call was made later that evening to Chikara Arakaki by an Israeli with a Moroccan accent. "I met Abe this evening and read him as what we Jews would call a mensch, a man of character."

"Thanks," Chikara said into the phone. "That's what I thought."

Abe and Adam attended services the next morning at the Chabad house, had lunch at the café, and ordered in for dinner that evening from the rabbi's son's kosher catering service. On Sunday, Kiyoko picked up Abe and Adam, then brought them to the Outrigger Club in Waikiki. Kiyoko's younger brother Yoshi had an outrigger canoe on the beach waiting for them. Abe was wearing a wide-brimmed fisherman's hat and wore an oversized boxy bathing suit and t-shirt. Adam was dressed in a similar fashion, wearing enough SP 50 sunblock to scare Herman Munster.

Yoshi gave Adam and Abe some paddles and a quick lesson in stroke technique and procedures. Yoshi was a fit young man in his early twenties with a perpetual smile on his face. He was the steersman at the rear of the canoe with two of his friends as the stroker in the first seat and the other in the second seat. Kiyoko was in the third seat with Abe and Adam in seats four and five.

"I hope you guys know how to swim in case this canoe hulis (flips) over," Yoshi said. "If it does, hang onto the boat. My friends and I will right the boat, so no worries. It won't happen. The waves are small today, but we are going to try to catch and ride some. It will be fun."

Adam said a quick prayer and whispered to Abe, "What did you get me into? The last time I was in the ocean was at Coney Island when I was five years old, and I was scared shitless then!"

Kiyoko, in a two-piece bathing suit and seated right in front of Abe, distracted his concentration on his paddling so much he screwed up the boat's forward progress. An outrigger canoe crew changes sides every twelve to fifteen strokes using a "hut" call to signal the change. Abe was in the number four seat, so he was supposed to match the strokes of the number two seat, but he screwed up the rhythm of the boat so badly that Yoshi had to stop the boat to get him back in sync.

Abe finally got the hang of it, and the canoe caught a small wave and rode it into the shore, with Yoshi doing a perfect pause at the end of the ride by turning the canoe around to try to catch another.

Abe muttered to himself, "I love this. I haven't had so

much fun since high school." He glanced at Adam, who was sweating profusely and looked like he was back on the Coney Island Cyclone about to hurtle down the first monster hill.

On Monday morning, Abe and Adam met Chikara and Kazuo at the store. Chikara announced that he had a proposal regarding the purchase that might just work. Adam met with Kazuo for about thirty minutes, and both came out smiling.

The deal was consummated, and a consulting agreement and a profit-sharing agreement were made for the initial eighteen months. It was a win/win solution. Adam and Abe were quite surprised at the turnaround by Chikara and Kazuo.

After they left the shop, Abe and Adam looked at each other in amazement. "Abe, Baruch Hashem, it looks like we bought Shaloha Gems!"

ADAM AND ABE returned to New York to commence the process of listing Goldy's diamond retail business. Goldstein's wholesale business would remain with his family, including his relatives who were the diamond cutters in Haifa. Abe's parents were shocked at his decision to pack up and leave New York City and go halfway across the world to the middle of the Pacific Ocean to set up a business in what they considered a foreign country.

Abe's mother was particularly upset. "Where are you going to find a Jewish girl on that rock a million miles away? Are there any Jews there?"

"Of course, Ma," Abe said placatingly. "There is a Chabad house in Honolulu with a large Israeli population.

I'll be going to the West Coast on business trips. There's a huge Jewish community in Los Angeles."

She crossed her arms, jaw tight. "Abe, it's just not a place for a single Jewish man."

Abe's father, Moishe, was also upset. "Abe-Ala, I do not have many years left. I want to see my son as much as I can before I go. "

"Pop, I will come home at least twice a year, and you and Ma should come to Hawaii at least once a year in the wintertime and stay for a month or longer. You would love it. I have a kosher caterer already lined up."

Abe's father snorted with derision. "Nah, this whole idea is meshuga. Your mother's right. It is not a place for a single Jewish man. You are never going to get married living there, and you will deny your poor mother the chance to have some grandchildren."

Abe decided to change tacks. "Mom, Pop, I want to get out of New York," he said seriously. "You yourselves know it's become a toilet and a dangerous toilet at that. Hawaii is warm, safe, and beautiful. There's a potentially great business opportunity there and room for expansion and we came up with a great name." He spread his arms wide, as they both gave him mutinous stares. "Shaloha Gems!"

CHAPTER 3
MOISHE'S JOURNEY

After the liberation of Dachau, Moishe was sent to a displaced persons camp in Salzburg, Austria. He spent six months there in what was called a transient camp named New Palestine run by the United Nations Relief and Rehabilitation Association with the assistance of the American Joint Distribution Committee.

In December 1945, President Truman loosened the quota on displaced persons immigrating to the United States under the Displaced Person's Act of 1948. It allowed 200,000 refugees to enter the United States. Some 28,000 of them were displaced survivors from the concentration camps. As the ships arrived in New York Harbor in March 1949, the refugees were seen openly weeping when they passed the Statue of Liberty.

After living below deck in steerage for almost two weeks during the trip across the Atlantic, Moishe could not believe his eyes as he came up to the ship's top deck. Leaning on the railing and looking at the giant buildings of New York City, he thought about what his father once told him about America: "Moishela, America is gut tzu Yiddin." *America is good to the Jews.*

As the ship docked at the intake center at Ellis Island, the refugees were interviewed by immigration officials with assistance from volunteers from Jewish agencies. Moishe's relatives had arranged that a representative from the Jewish agency bring Moishe through immigration. After two hours, a very tired Moishe finally met his distant relatives, who hugged and kissed the skinny teenager. It was the first time Moishe had been hugged since his father gave him his last parting hug at Dachau.

Zelman Goldstein and his brother Neil Goldstein, who both had eaten one kugel too many, had a small shop called Goldy's Diamonds near the Diamond Dealers Club at Thirty West 47th Street where major disputes were settled. The block of West 47th Street from Fifth Avenue to the Avenue of the Americas is the heart of the nation's multibillion-dollar diamond business. The Street of Diamonds is where the bulk of all the diamonds in America are originally sold.

Even back then, the grimy stores were ablaze with gems. The offices upstairs also contained millions of dollars' worth of diamonds. This is where shabby-looking Orthodox brokers bickered over a pittance before agreeing to million-dollar deals on a handshake.

The Diamond District was a bizarre world that combined the crassness of Old-World shtetl street peddlers with a strict code of honor. The "Mazal and Bracha" (good luck and blessings) phrase used to seal diamond deals, followed by a handshake, this is how one conducts business in the NY diamond business. A man's word was his bond. It was a world within itself, a bazaar of precious stones and negotiations in many languages more than one thousand years in the making. It had been molded from centuries of persecution, pogroms, forced emigrations, and concentration camps to form a tight community suspicious of strangers because of their tragic history. Moishe was thrown into this intense scene where everyone was buying and/or selling diamonds.

At first, Moishe ran errands for Zelman and Neil. He mostly went out to get coffee. Then he would run to Neil's apartment and pick up sandwiches from Neil's wife Sadie or ride the subway downtown to Katz's Deli and pick up pastrami sandwiches. When Zelman realized that Moishe was good with numbers, he had him sit in on negotiations on purchases.

"Moishela," Zelman said. "You got a Yiddisha kop for numbers, boychik, be on the lookout for deals. If you can find deals for us, we will give you a 5 percent referral fee. But no treif (non-Kosher) deals, got it?"

Moishe spent over a year watching his cousin's deal-making and worked with Neil on the classification of gems and how to recognize their quality. Eventually, he graduated from being an errand boy to a courier of small gems from one dealer to another. He began to travel downtown to Canal Street and to the shops on the Lower East Side to trade gems.

He made a few small diamond deals at first with low-level dealers. In his dealings with a wealthy merchant named Haim Shapiro on 47th Street, he noticed Haim's pretty daughter, Miriam. When Moishe made inquiries about Miriam he was told that a shidduch (a matchmaking arrangement) had already been set up with a yeshiva scholar. However, Miriam was hard-headed and went against the plan, which was a Shonda or disgrace to their family. After the engagement fell apart, Miriam would occasionally flirt with Moishe. From then on, he made a lot of excuses to visit Haim's shop.

Moishe had no standing or money to court Miriam, so he was determined to change that one way or another. He worked hard to recognize good deals and brought those to Zelman and Neil. At one point, Moishe realized that he could handle and negotiate the deal himself, and he saved all of his referral fees to buy a stone for himself. Only if the deal was big would he go into partnership with his relatives.

When he traveled with stones, he always wore a hollowed-out leather belt with small packets under his tzitzi strings that contained the gems. He would also wear a jacket with the standard diamond dealer vest that would contain a gem holder where the inexpensive gems would be kept in case of a robbery.

One day in the early evening, he was leaving after a Canal Street purchase for Zelman and Neil when he heard screams in an alleyway. Moise cautiously ran to where the screams came from and witnessed a Black man running from the scene. A Hasidic diamond dealer whom he knew as a *goniff*, a swindler and cheat, was lying in a pool of blood in the alley with his jacket open, bleeding from multiple stab wounds. Having witnessed death firsthand in the camps, he didn't panic at the sight and recognized right away that the man was dead. Moishe said a Hebrew prayer. Then he noticed that the man's "vest" was missing.

The thief must have stolen his diamonds, thought Moishe, but on a hunch, he checked under his tzitzit strings for a belt similar to the one he himself wore. He pulled the belt off, felt it, and realized that it was filled with gems. He put the bloody belt on while looking for a payphone to call the NYPD. Moishe did not identify himself in the call, but described the assailant, and did not hang around to be interviewed by the police. He proceeded uptown to his room that he rented from his relatives.

The murder was reported in the local Yiddish-language newspaper and *The New York Post*. The murdered dealer was buried within twenty-four hours, as required by Jewish law, and his funeral was attended by many in the Diamond District, including Zelman and Neil. An NYPD message was sent out in the Yiddish-language paper for the witness to come forth and provide information on the assailant. Moishe realized that if he did, the police would question him as a potential suspect. If he surfaced with an extraordinary number of stones, people would whisper and likely even accuse him of the murder.

In the old country, Jews rarely dealt with the police. They were notoriously anti-Semitic and were looked upon as an enemy. In the privacy of his bedroom, Moishe opened up the money belt and scattered the gems on his desk. He used a jeweler's loupe to examine them closely. Moishe estimated that there were over $400,000 to $500,000 worth of gems. Many of the gems were in the two and three karat range.

Moishe prayed to God for guidance. He remembered when he was in the camps and despairing, telling his father that he no longer wanted to live. In the camps, when another inmate died, everyone ransacked his or her body and belongings for any leftover food or warm clothing for their survival. His survival instincts were what had kept him alive, ingrained in Moishe like the number on his arm.

Moishe recalled his father's words. "You have to live; you can't let these bastards win. You must survive and have children. Hashem will take care of you, my son. You might not believe it now, but he will."

Hashem had spared him and had now given him this gift to change his life. He would keep the gems for his own but give *tzedakah* (charity) and pray for forgiveness every Yom Kippur. Moishe realized that he needed to move these gems slowly and make it look like it was in the normal course of business with others outside of the Diamond District. He would move the smaller gems first since the larger diamonds would arouse suspicion so soon after the crime.

Moishe rented a small safe deposit box in a guarded vault located beneath a building on the corner of 47th Street and Fifth Avenue. The facility was secured with 24-hour guards and was private. Moishe loaded the gems into the safe, keeping the smaller one-karat diamonds to sell.

A month later Moishe read in the Yiddish newspaper that the murderer had been apprehended. The word on 47th St. was that the killer was arrested when he tried to sell the stolen gems to an NYPD informant who was a known fence for stolen jewelry. A search warrant on the man's apartment revealed the bloody vest taken from the victim with the blood stains matching that of the deceased.

Moishe, who by now was twenty-one years old, approached Zelman and Neil with a proposal. "Cousin Zelman, I thank you so much for allowing me to learn and work with you and Neil. However, I would like to rent a small cubicle at the diamond exchange for a couple of days a week to start my own business. I would like to work with you on deals and continue to work in your office three or four days a week, but I think it's time I build my own business."

"That is ambitious of you," Zelman said, "but we had

plans for you to work with our son-in-law Mendel to take over our business. You have a good head on your shoulders, and Mendel is not a *gaon* (genius)."

"I thought so too, but I am interested in a maidel (single woman) and her father will not allow me to court her unless I am staked and have a successful business."

"Then I understand, Moishela. Yes, you can rent a cubicle at the diamond exchange. Mazel tov!"

Moishe thought the best way to move the larger gems was through foreign buyers such as the new group of Indian diamond dealers in the city, whose companies were based in India. He met Babu Singh, a dark, bespeckled Sikh who wore a red turban and sported a full beard. Babu had a cubicle near his at the Diamond Exchange. Babu represented a large diamond family in Bombay, so Moishe set up a meeting with him outside of the Diamond District at a Lower East Side hotel away from the eyes of any Orthodox dealers.

Moishe and Babu drank tea and exchanged pleasantries. Babu was one of the first Indians to be allowed into the mostly Orthodox Jewish diamond exchange. Indians were taking a lot of business from the traditional dealers and moved other gems as well as diamonds, including rubies and sapphires. The Sikhs were monotheists and believed in one God, most Indians, being Hindus, were looked upon by the orthodox jewish community as idol worshippers, not to be trusted — and for whom Mazal and Bracha did not apply.

However, Moishe and Babu became friends, and often joked with each other since they were situated in adjoining stalls at the exchange.

"Moishe, why do we have to meet away from the

exchange when our stalls are so close that we can spit and hit each other?" Babu wondered.

"To be honest, I'm trying to keep some transactions private since my relatives always want a percentage for themselves. These stones that I will show you I obtained myself with no help from my relatives. I love and respect them, but I need to build up an inventory of my own so I can have my own business someday. Any transactions with you must be in confidence."

Babu gave Moishe a conspiratorial look. *Why would Moishe not sell his stones to me at the exchange. Why out of sight of his colleagues and, most of all, his employers?*

Babu reflected that these stones were hot.

"Show me what you got," Babu said. "You did not bring me here to drink fine Ceylon tea, although I might have some fine Ceylon sapphires to sell or trade you."

Moishe had three three-carat diamonds in a white cloth that he laid on the table.

Babu took out his loupe and examined each pear-shaped stone carefully. "*Acha, behut acha* (good, very good). I'll give you $100,000 for all three."

Moishe, a trained gemologist, knew these three stones were flawless and top quality and could fetch $50,000 to $60,000 apiece. "Babu, you insult me. You know that these are worth at least $50,000 each."

Babu eyed him shrewdly. "There must be a reason that you are not selling them at the exchange. Why are you meeting me with no prying eyes? I can only imagine why — although on second thought, I don't care where these stones came from as long as I get a good price. $120,000. Take it or leave it."

"I'll take it if you throw in three one-karat velvet blue

color natural sapphires. Babu, I know you can source these through Sri Lanka. I have a client that is very interested in velvet blue sapphires. You are still getting a bargain on this, and this can open up a new market for you amongst my network, many of whom won't do business with an Indian but will trust me. I will work exclusively with you Babu." He held up his palms. "Look at it as a door opener."

"Acha, Moishe, behut acha," Babu grumbled after a moment. "Fine, but I'll trade you two sapphires, not three."

This transaction staked Moishe for other purchases of perfect one-karat diamonds that were much easier to move on the retail market and began his strategic partnership with Babu. Eventually, he acquired a reputation on 47th Street and began a full partnership with his cousins, Zelman and Neil.

At last, Moishe felt that it was time to ask for the hand of the lovely and headstrong Miriam Shapiro, whom he still occasionally saw at her father's shop. He went to a matchmaker who proposed a shidduch. Miriam's parents approved of the match since Moishe had built a reputation as a successful businessman and a righteous person who gave tzedakah to the synagogue. Moishe and Miriam were married in a traditional orthodox ceremony.

A few years after their marriage, they had a baby boy named Abe. He was named after Moishe's father who died at Dachau. After the birth, Moishe said a prayer at the Lubavitch headquarters at 770 Ocean Parkway in Brooklyn for his father, he had a lump in his throat as he whispered the words.

"Baruch Hashem, Pop, we beat the evil ones that tried to kill us. Like our diamonds, our family line will be forever."

CHAPTER 4
A CHERRY BLOSSOM PASSOVER

Adam came into Abe's office late one sunny morning, the trademark sly grin on his face.

"So, how are your parents taking it, Abe?"

Abe looked up from his desk with a welcoming smile. "Bombastic, they're taking it as well as if I just announced that I joined the Hare Krishnas, shaved my head, and was running off to India. By the way, since you're coming with me for at least three to six months, how does your wife feel about that?"

Adam dropped into a chair and sighed. "I think that she's secretly happy to get rid of me, but of course won't admit it. I notice that she's been singing to herself while doing housework for the first time in years."

"Bombastic, I think that's a hint."

AFTER THE COMMERCIAL real estate agent listed the property, offers began to come in. Finally, another existing diamond dealer made a serious offer. Within three days of negotiation, the New York business was sold.

Abe and Adam caught a flight back to Honolulu a week after the closing. They got a limo and checked into the Royal Hawaiian, an older but classic Waikiki landmark pink-colored hotel. After coffee, they dropped into the Aloha Diamond store and began listing the inventory that was incorporated into the sale. After a few hours of work, with a lot more to do, they called it quits and went back to their hotel.

Kiyoko called Abe and invited him to the Cherry Blossom Queen festival ball sponsored by the Japanese Junior chamber of commerce the next evening, advising that "we are, and you will be a sponsor for this event. You wanted to learn Japanese culture and more importantly local Hawaiian politics. This will be the best place to start."

"I'd love to," he replied warmly, imagining a pleasant, perhaps even romantic evening with beautiful Kiyoko.

"Go to the drugstore," she continued, "get a Covid test kit, and test yourself and Adam tomorrow before the 5:00 p.m. pageant since the JJCC requires a negative test at least 48 hours before attending. Then take a picture of your negative test next to your digital watch to confirm the date the test was taken."

Abe threw his hands up. "But Kiyoko, I've had two shots and a booster. Isn't that enough?"

"Not for the Japanese Junior Chamber of commerce," she said sternly. "That's why at the peak of this pandemic the Japanese tourists visiting the US had to go to quarantine prison for two weeks, even if they had been vaccinated. Same mentality. Acquiescence to authority, lots of social pressure to obey and conform."

"Okay," he said dryly, "I surrender."

To Abe's amusement and consternation, she sent two aloha shirts and two matching flowered yarmulkes to their hotel to wear to the pageant. She met both men at the Sheraton Waikiki Hotel within sight of the event, where they checked in.

Since Kiyoko and her father were longtime sponsors, they had tables near the stage. Chikara was recognized by the MC as a gold-level sponsor, and he stood up and waved to the audience.

The pageant was quite impressive. A local weatherman was the MC, and the program began with a Taiko drumming performance that was so loud it almost blew Adam's yarmulke off. The next portion was the introduction of the contestants, who wore the exact same evening gown. All gave a short speech about themselves, their struggles, and their outlook. All were optimistic, describing challenges related to their family — and all struck Abe as coming from the same cookie-cutter mold.

Kiyoko was seated between Adam and Abe. Abe shared his observation with her. "Kiyoko, these girls were beautiful and feminine, but their stories were so similar and conforming."

"Abe, in traditional Japanese culture, the concept of *Iijime* (ee-jee-may) translates into beating down the nail that sticks up. Conformity is the standard. Less so here in Hawaii where the concept is more relaxed, but it is still expected behavior."

He nodded as the girls filed off the stage. Kiyoko leaned over. "There is also a personality trait that Japanese women think is attractive to men," she whispered. "They always want to be *kawaii*, which means cute. Japanese women aspire to be cute. That's what they think men want."

Abe chuckled. "Kiyoko, Jewish women aspire to be provocative and sometimes argumentative, especially if others do not agree with their politics, which is why so many become lawyers or marry lawyers.

"If there were a Jewish Junior Chamber of Commerce with Jewish women in a beauty contest, no one would win," he said. "There would probably be a catfight back-stage over who went out first, and half of the women would speak about being social justice warriors to fight racism, homophobia, and climate change."

Adam nodded sagely. "You can bet a lawsuit would be filed in the aftermath about something."

During the intermission and dinner break, Kenji Ono, the slick, well-dressed owner of Ono Diamonds, dropped by the table and said hello to Kiyoko.

"Ogenki desu ka?" he asked politely. *How are you?*

Kiyoko replied, "Genki desu, Kenji-San." *I'm fine.*

Her father, Chikara, would not even acknowledge his presence since there was so much bad blood between them over the years.

"I hear you are selling your business," Kenji said to Kiyoko with a stiff smile. "Congratulations, are these two gentlemen the buyers?"

"Yes, they are," she replied. "Kenji, this is Abe, and this is Adam."

The men shook hands. "Welcome to Hawaii, you guys from New York?"

"Yep, we are, Kenji," said Abe.

"New York Jews, huh?"

Abe pretended amazement. "Kenji, you are one sharp cookie. The yarmulkes must have given us away."

Adam chimed in, "They aren't really yarmulkes.

They're round face masks, and we didn't know what to do with them during dinner."

Kenji gave them both a sarcastic smirk and walked away. Abe and Adam glanced at each other and whispered, "Schmuck."

During intermission, Kiyoko brought Adam and Abe over to the table of another sponsor, the Oshiro wedding company, and introduced them to a distinguished Japanese gentleman about eighty years of age. Kiyoko spoke to him in Japanese while Mr. Oshiro bowed to Abe and Adam, obviously being told that they were the new owners. In broken English, he congratulated them and said he wanted to continue their business relationship.

When they went back to the table, Kiyoko told Abe that this little Japanese man ran a one-hundred-million-dollar a year business setting up weddings for Japanese people and had seventy offices in Japan that solicited business. "He has been gracious to our business over the years by allowing us to advertise in his flyers and on his television show in Japan," she said. "We work with tour operators to send their visitors to our store, and we treat them well by setting up special showings for preferred guests."

Next on the agenda was a kimono dress competition and the crowning of the Cherry Blossom Queen. A Japanese girl who, in Abe's humble opinion, was not even close to being the best-looking was chosen to be the Cherry Blossom Queen. Abe mentioned this to Kiyoko, who explained that she was the daughter of a prominent family who contributes a lot to the JJCC.

"Which is the way things work over here," she added wryly.

The next day was Friday. Adam and Abe met Kiyoko and

her brother Kazuo at the office in the morning. After some paperwork, they broke for lunch at the Shalom Café, and Abe attempted to explain the concept of kosher food to her.

"Kiyoko, according to our bible, we are forbidden to eat meat from animals that do not have split hooves and chew their cud."

When she frowned in confusion, he gave an example: a pig has split hooves but does not chew his cud, whereas cows both chew their cud and have split hooves.

"There is also a requirement for the kosher humane slaughter of animals so as not to cause the animal too much suffering. If you ask me for an explanation, the only one that I can give you is that God said it in the Torah, the Jewish bible. There are other restrictions, like not eating milk with meat, and it can get complicated."

Kiyoko asked, "I understand that you cannot eat certain types of seafood, like shrimp or lobster?"

"Yes, you are correct, Kiyoko. We can eat anything from the sea that has both scales and fins. Lobsters, shrimp, and crabs do not, so we cannot eat them."

"What about *tako*, octopus? Can you eat that?"

He shook his head. "No scales, no fins, so we can't eat them, nor can we eat squid."

Kiyoko seemed confused and yet fascinated. "These rules come from your Torah. I have read up about it since meeting you. I understand that it is over three thousand years old."

"Kiyoko, in a few weeks, we celebrate Passover, which commemorates the Hebrews' exodus from Egypt after enslavement for four hundred years. We observe the holiday by conducting a seder dinner. If you would like, I will invite you to attend one at the Chabad house."

A few weeks later, after Adam and Abe worked

through the inventory and meetings were held with tour operators and others in the wedding industry, Kiyoko explained that "these relationships have been built over two generations by my father and grandfather. You will have to maintain them, and we will help you, but these relationships can be lost very quickly if not handled correctly and if our partners are not shown the proper respect."

On the evening of the first night of Passover, Adam and Abe met Kiyoko in the lobby of the Chabad house, the orthodox Jewish congregation where Abe and Adam attended services. A uniformed police officer was stationed in the lobby to provide security for the service and the ensuing seder dinner.

Abe and Adam already attended services at the synagogue located on the penthouse, with the seder dinner on the ground floor.

"Abe, is there always a policeman at these dinners? Why do you need them?"

"Kiyoko, there is only security during major holidays. Since Passover is a major holiday, it becomes a target for people that hate us, so it's better to be careful, and it makes the people here feel more secure."

Abe, Adam, and Kiyoko seated themselves at an assigned table with a mix of Israelis and American Jews. Smatterings of Hebrew and New York-accented English flavored the conversation, and all the men wore kippahs or yarmulkes. Many of them spoke over each other. Some were arguing, sometimes loudly. It reminded Kiyoko of the movie *Annie Hall* when Woody Allen invited his WASP girlfriend to dinner at his family's house under the Coney Island roller coaster.

The Rabbi started the seder, which translates to order.

"The seder has an order of fifteen rituals, which includes saying the blessing over wine and the matzah as well as the ritual washing of the hands."

Kiyoko expressed interest in the reasons for the rituals and the specific blessings, so Abe explained that through almost two thousand years of the Jewish diaspora living in exile from their promised land, the Torah, the first five books of the Hebrew Bible, and these religious rituals remained the same. "They kept the continuity of the religion going through thousands of years of turmoil, displacement, and destruction," he said.

As Kiyoko nodded, clearly moved by these ancient, sacred traditions, Adam chimed in, "The history of the Jews is, basically, they tried to kill us, we survived, let's eat!"

CHAPTER 5
ABIE'S OKINAWAN ROSE

Over the next few weeks, Abe and Adam worked with Kiyoko and her brother, Kazuo, and occasionally her father, Chikara, to examine the cash flow, inventory, and strategic partners.

A meeting was held with Mr. Oshiro's wedding company. He indicated that they would continue the business relationship, and that would include advertising on their wedding website in Japan with discounts on diamond engagement and wedding rings for their wedding packages.

At the meeting, Kiyoko brought gifts for all the attendees. Lots of bowing and deference were shown on both sides. However, Abe and Adam were not expected to participate in the bowing and formal greetings. Kiyoko clued them in as far as what to do. Oshiro's son Taka ran the meeting and, at the conclusion, invited Abe and Kiyoko to lunch at a traditional Japanese restaurant where Taka had already made a reservation. Kiyoko responded that Abe and Adam would love to attend but, because of their religious dietary restrictions, could not join the others for lunch. Taka was disappointed but said he understood.

Afterward, Kiyoko gently explained to Abe and Adam that it was very much a Japanese tradition to eat and drink with business associates.

"In Japan, it is customary to have a *nijikai*, a second meeting after the formal business meeting, where the participants let down their hair, make small talk, and after a few drinks really get down to business," she said. "What I suggest you do is rent a suite at a hotel, cater the food and drink with a kosher caterer, and have the nijikai then. By renting a suite at a five-star hotel, you would be showing them big face, which is exactly what you want to do to begin this very important relationship."

The two men shared a look and nodded. "It's a win-win solution," Abe said. "Thank you, Kiyoko."

She gave him a warm smile. "Abe, I'm going to start to try to teach you some basic Japanese for business. Again, when you attempt to speak the language, the Japanese are flattered by your efforts, again showing them big face. You should also try Duolingo or even Rosetta Stone, which will help you to read Japanese hiragana and katakana."

Later that day, Kiyoko met Abe at a local Starbucks and logged into a Japanese-language website. Since Abe spoke three languages — English, Hebrew, and Yiddish (which is a derivation of German) — he picked up Japanese much more quickly than most.

Abe couldn't help but notice how patient Kiyoko was in teaching him, exhibiting no frustration with his dumb mistakes, providing constant encouragement and gentle correction. When they left Starbucks and came to a cross-walk, the pedestrian signal was red, but there were no cars for blocks in either direction. Abe looked both ways and started crossing the street. Kiyoko dutifully stayed at the curb, waiting for the light to change.

"Abe, what are you doing?" she called, hurrying after him once it turned green. "The light was red!"

He shrugged. "Kiyoko, there were no cars in sight. Why should we wait at a crosswalk when it's totally safe, and you can simply walk across? No one cares."

Her eyes narrowed. "Abe, that's jaywalking in Hawaii, and you can be fined."

He looked around at the empty streets. "Kiyoko, no one is here to see us jaywalk. Only we would know."

"Abe, I know, but that's the way I was raised — to obey all authority, even if it's just a streetlight."

He swallowed a laugh. Kiyoto looked perfectly serious. "Wow, in New York, if you did that, everyone would think you were meshuga, crazy."

Her voice was slightly cool. "Abe, people here would think you were an A-hole mainland *haole* (white foreigner) if you jaywalked like that. Remember Ijma (ee-jee-may), the nail that sticks up gets beaten down? You can't come across as going against the grain, being too aggressive, especially with mainland Japanese as well as locals. Here you will get stink-eye." She demonstrated with an exaggerated hostile stare. Abe laughed and the tension broke.

"Point taken," he conceded. "When in Rome . . ."

They walked through Kapi'olani Park. As they were walking, Kiyoko noticed that a baby bird had fallen from a tree. She gently nestled the baby mynah bird in a tissue from her purse and brought the bird into her car.

"I've nursed baby birds before and don't have a great track record in keeping them alive," she admitted ruefully, "but I have to try. Poor little thing."

Abe nodded approval. "Trying to save the bird is what

the Jews would call a mitzvah. An act of kindness or chari-ty," he said, adding that "saving a human life is the greatest mitzvah of all."

Abe was more and more taken by her, her beauty, kind-ness, grace, and femininity. She was unlike any woman he had ever met.

Before they parted, he mentioned to Kiyoko that it was his turn to be the sensei or teacher. Kiyoko told him that she had been learning about Judaism on her own so that she could better understand her new business partners.

When Abe got back to the condo that he and Adam were renting, he found his friend sitting there with his head in his hands, looking distressed.

"Sarah filed for divorce. I got a letter from a lawyer today claiming abandonment. As you know, I have been miserable for years, as I am sure she has been as well, but this is still a body blow." He shook his head, eyes glazed with shock. "To be honest with you, in a way I'm relieved since I knew this day would come, but still, it's hard to take."

Abe's heart went out to him. He laid a hand on his shoulder. "Adam, you have the right to want to be happy. Hashem wants you to be happy." He sighed. "Not to distract from your bad news, but I'm afraid that I am falling for Kiyoko. I cannot get her out of my mind. Do you think I am meshuga to fall for her?"

Adam gave a wry smile. "You just answered your own question, Abe."

Sudden doubts crept in. "I don't even know if she has any feelings for me. I could be fooling myself."

"Hey Abe-Ala, do you think that she wants to study Judaism so she can learn about Jewish dietary laws? She is doing this so she can get closer to you, get it?"

His spirits lifted. "Do you really think so, Adam? "

"Abe, I picked up on that when we first started this. She's got something for you, I'm telling you, pal."

He beamed. "Baruch Hashem." (God's blessings)

KIYOKO ENROLLED in online courses through the Jewish Learning Center and read about the Torah, the Talmud, and Kabbalah. Most of it was confusing to her, and she discussed some of the concepts with Abe. Abe would attempt to explain things to Kiyoko. She found the concept of mitzvot (doing good deeds) as being similar in a reverse kind of way to the Japanese concept of *bachi* — the idea that something bad will happen to you if your actions are malicious.

In essence, what goes around comes around.

As with most Okinawan Japanese, religion was not a large part of her life. She was a member of the Okinawan American Association and occasionally went to a Hong-wanji temple to light a fu stick and chant a prayer when someone got seriously ill. But that and participating in the Obon festival to celebrate their ancestors during the harvest moon in August was the extent of her religious activity.

Kiyoko was drawn to learning about Judaism and was also drawn closer to Abe as he explained this 3,000-year-old religion. She also appreciated his willingness to temper his sometimes loud and aggressive behavior with vendors that the Arakaki family had built long-term relationships with over the years.

Abe would watch from a distance when the sales staff would deal with a customer and politely come in at the end and offer them tea or a small present, politely stating *Sumimasen* (excuse me) and *Dozo irasshai* as he presented the small gift to the customer. Kiyoko would offer compliments and suggestions on how well he handled the interaction. However, Abe realized that it was essential that he retain the Arakaki sales staff to make this business a success.

At one point, Abe caught Covid and was isolated in his apartment. Kiyoko insisted on visiting and brought therapeutic treatments that she obtained through her long-term family doctor. She even brought Abe kosher chicken soup, a.k.a., "Jewish penicillin." From the Shalom Café. He could tell that she was really concerned about him, and he sent flowers to thank her. He even wrote a note that said, "To my Okinawan Rose, Love, Abe."

That note broke the ice on their relationship.

After Abe got better and tested negative, they took long walks together near the ocean, occasionally holding hands.

"Kiyoko, I would never do this at home," he confessed. "My orthodox community would frown on it, but you know what? I don't really care."

She squeezed his hand. "Abe, you are not at home. You are in Hawaii. This will *become* your home."

They even went to the beach once on a break from the office on a Friday afternoon.

"Abe, it's Aloha Friday. Here in Hawaii, most people skip out of work early on Friday afternoon and have a long weekend. It's Pau Hana — the workday is over." She grinned teasingly. "You have to learn about Hawaiian culture as well as Japanese culture."

"Kiyoko, I want to start advertising here in the islands. Hopefully, we can attract clients from all the islands interested in engagement and wedding rings." He struck a pose, hands on hips. "Do you think that local people would want to see a Jewish guy with a yarmulke in a commercial?"

She grinned. "I don't see why not? We have a Jewish US senator and a lieutenant governor, both married to Asians. "

Abe and Kiyoko worked together grading their diamond stock and repricing some gems for the grand opening of Shaloha Gems. Abe would bring his kosher lunch to work every day and Kiyoko would go out for "plate lunch," which was usually chicken katsu or pulled pork with two scoops of white rice and one scoop of macaroni salad. On Saturdays, since Abe could not work on the sabbath, he would meet Kiyoko after his morning prayers at Kapi'olani Park under a huge 150-year-old banyan tree and they'd eat their lunches watching children play in the park.

"Kiyoko, the atmosphere here is so relaxed," he said. "I must get used to this pace. In New York we were always in a mad rush. I think my blood pressure has dropped twenty points since I got here, but how can you stay motivated when you can just take off from work and go surfing?"

He'd been half-joking, but Kiyoko took the question seriously — a trait he admired about her. She leaned back against the bench and crossed her slender ankles, gazing out across the wide emerald lawns.

"These kids also smoke *pakalolo*, locally grown very potent marijuana, on a regular basis, which further kills their motivation," she said. "By the time they are in their twenties most of them are working service industry jobs, sometimes two or three jobs to make ends meet. They can't afford to buy a home so they either live at home in houses purchased by their grandparents or rent with others, and never have any ambition to do anything else but surf and smoke dope. You are lucky to get an employee to show up on time — or sometimes, to show up at all."

Abe finished his lunch and tucked the trash in a bag. "My father was very strict. Only my younger brother Yoshi would go astray and rebel. He's a good kid but not very motivated to work, which drives my father crazy." Abe exhaled a long breath. The happy shrieks of the children playing seemed to fade as the weight of the past cast a shadow over their picnic.

"Kiyoko, my father was liberated from a German concentration camp. The Germans murdered his entire family. It's something that lives with you forever. Not a lot of happy memories from his childhood, he started from nothing in New York City. Luckily, his distant American relatives took him in and brought him into their business. He hustled to build his own business, ended up buying out his relatives' company, then greatly expanded its connections in South Africa, Israel, India, and Australia. Failure was not an option for him. He pushed me hard, sometimes too much. He was driven to succeed and made sure that I did."

Tears welled up in Kiyoko's eyes and she reached out to touch his hand. "I'm sorry to hear that Abe, it makes me sad. We had relatives in Okinawa who also suffered greatly during the war. One of our relatives named Tomiko wrote a book about her experiences. She was only six years old when the battle of Okinawa happened in 1945. She fled with her mother and two sisters, living in caves on the island, scavenging for food from vegetable plots and from the knapsacks of dead soldiers. Her mother was killed by bombs when she left the cave to get food. Young Tomiko got separated from her sisters and found a cave that was occupied by an elderly couple who fed and cared for her.

"One day in June 1945 they heard Americans talking outside the cave, calling in Japanese for them to surrender. The older couple, thinking that if they did not come out the Americans would burn them to death with fire, sent little Tomiko out holding a white flag. She expected to be killed by these people who she was told were barbarians.

"The three American soldiers, one of whom was taking pictures, were kind and fed the little girl and the elderly couple in the cave. Years later as an adult she saw her image in a photo book about the war and decided to write a book about her experiences called 'The Girl with the White Flag.' She tracked down the army photographer who took her picture and they had a reunion in Texas. An amazing and sad story."

Tears pricked Abe's own eyes. "Kiyoko, both of our families have seen much tragedy. We are worlds apart in our culture and religion, but I feel drawn to you since I have never met anyone as kind and sincere as you are." Abe reached out and held Kiyoko under the shade of the banyan tree.

She snuggled against him. "Traditional Buddhism believes that Siddhartha, the Buddha, meditated under a Bodhi tree until he reached enlightenment. Maybe we are reaching something like enlightenment between us?"

His lips curled in a smile against her hair. "I'm not sure if its enlightenment, and I'm definitely not the Buddha, but whatever it is I like it."

"I like it too Abe," she said, as they kissed under the banyan tree.

ONE DAY, as they strolled through a local botanical garden in Manoa Valley Park, they passed a huge, beautiful cherry blossom tree in full bloom.

Abe mentioned to Kiyoko, "Wow, what a beautiful tree. Why do the Japanese revere it?"

"This tree is supposed to signify the beauty and fragility of life. When it blooms, it signifies happiness and a fresh start in life. It means enjoy your life now since, like the cherry blossom, it will not last too long."

Abe nodded. "Like the cherry blossom, our lives are short, we only have one chance, our feelings for each other are real, and like the cherry blossom, we must grasp it before life fades."

At that moment, Abe gently held Kiyoko and gave her a kiss. Kiyoko kissed him back.

"Well, if a US senator and lieutenant governor are married to an Asian, maybe a Jewish diamond merchant needs to be married to an Asian as well," he ventured, sudden nerves fluttering his stomach. "Would you consider marrying a New York Jewish guy that wears a funny hat, eats strange food, and doesn't turn on the lights on Friday night to Saturday evening, but will love you forever?"

She threw her arms around his neck, eyes shining. "Yes, Abe, I would marry you. Will your family accept me?"

His heart swelled with joy. "Kiyoko, I don't care. I'm the one marrying you. We deserve to be happy. Look at Adam. He's been miserable for years. His marriage was arranged, what is called a shidduch. Many in the orthodox community have arranged marriages. It keeps the culture alive."

Kiyoko smoothed a lock of curly hair back from his brow. "Strangely enough, about a third of marriages in

Japan are arranged as well, called *miai kekkon*." She giggled. "That is why the men are never home. They are either at work or getting drunk together at a bar."

He swallowed a fresh lump of worry. "Kiyoko, will your family accept me?"

"Abe, it will be difficult, but I will deal with it. I'm thirty-five years old, and I finally found someone I love. That is all that counts."

Abe and Kiyoko agreed that for now, their relationship should be kept secret so that the business relationship would not be jeopardized at the beginning stage of the partnership. They both agreed that this was not the right time to advise both of their families.

Back at the apartment, Abe told Adam about the proposal and acceptance.

"Adam, give me some advice. I love Kiyoko. What should I tell my family? How should I break it to them?"

Adam thought for a moment. "How about this? Ma, I have some great news! My brain tumor is benign! And by the way, I'm in love with a Japanese woman and want to get married."

CHAPTER 6
JEWISH /OKINAWAN ADVENTURE

Kiyoko took a course online through the Jewish Learning Institute, enrolling in Introduction to Judaism. Abe would sit with her and attempt to explain some of the basic concepts. He also made an appointment with Rabbi Shmuley to begin the conversion process.

They all met in the rabbi's office adjacent to the synagogue. It was somewhat messy and disorganized, with a prominent photograph on the wall behind his desk of a white-haired, white-bearded gentleman.

"Rabbi, who is this distinguished-looking man?" Kiyoko asked.

"This is the Rebbe Schneerson, who was the spiritual leader of the Chabad movement. He had the idea to send his emissaries, orthodox rabbis, to mentor the diaspora of Jews scattered throughout the world. To bring Jews back to Judaism. Chabad accepts anyone into the congregation. Many of our congregants are Jews, usually men, who marry non-Jews, and in Hawaii usually Asian women who sometimes convert to Judaism. The process is not easy, and it is meant to discourage those who are not committed to converting."

The Rabbi regarded her seriously. "Kiyoko, why do you want to want to convert to my religion besides the fact that you love Abe and want to marry him?"

"Rabbi, I was raised Shinto Buddhist through the Hongwanji temple here in Honolulu with spiritual connections to Okinawa. Most Japanese or Okinawans in Hawaii have a minimal connection to religion and only go to the temple on rare occasions. My grandparents had a *Butsudan*, a spirit house where there is a Buddha and pictures of diseased ancestors. We light fu sticks and chant prayers to honor our ancestors. But I always thought that there was something missing, a kind of void that I did not know how to fill."

He steepled his hands on the desk. "Kiyoko, the Jews would consider that idol worship, which is forbidden under the laws in our Torah. For conversion to Orthodox Judaism, you have to adhere to kashrut (kosher food) and keep the Shabbat, the sabbath, from sundown Friday evening to Saturday evening at sundown.

"It is a huge commitment and dominates your life. You have to think about how it will impact the life you have been living. What do your parents and family think about your relationship with Abe and your intention to convert?"

She glanced at Abe. "Rabbi, to be honest with you, we haven't told either of our parents. We realize that this relationship would not be welcomed in either of our families, and we were trying to find the right time to tell them."

The Rabbi frowned. "Kiyoko, I think that you should advise both of your families and gauge their reaction before you start the conversion process."

Abe gave this conversation a lot of thought. In the end, he skipped Adam's suggestion to tell his mother that the "brain tumor" was benign and, while she was recovering with joy, dropping the nuke on her. Like a visit to the oral surgeon, better to get it over with and hope for the best.

"Ma, I've got something to tell you and Pop."

"What? Are you going to tell me that you changed your mind? And that you are going to move back to New York or to Miami? Is it your health? Your father has a heart condition. You know it runs in the family!"

"Well, Ma, are you sitting down?" He drew a deep breath.

"Yes, what are you going to tell me?" A note of suspicion now. "That you decided you are gay? God forbid."

"No, Ma, I'm getting married. I found someone that I love, and we want to get married."

"Abe, you met this girl in Hawaii. Did you meet her at Chabad?" she asked with a hopeful tone. He heard her calling his father. "Moishe, Moishe, come listen! Abe is getting married. This is wonderful, wonderful. So, you met her at Chabad. Is she from there?"

"No, ma, I didn't meet her in Chabad. I met her through my jewelry business. She's a certified gemologist."

"That's wonderful. Where was she raised?"

"Hawaii, she and her entire family for generations are from Hawaii."

A distinctly cooler tone. "Abe, so you are telling me she's not Jewish. Is she Christian?"

"Not exactly Ma, she's an Okinawan Japanese, and her family is Buddhist."

Total silence on the line. Abe could hear his mother breathing heavily.

"Oh my god, Moishe, Moishe, you are not going to believe this! Your son is marrying an Oriental."

"Miriam, what did you say?" Abe's father erupted in the background. "Is he marrying a Chinese who worships idols?"

"Tell Pop she's Japanese Okinawan and is interested in converting."

"Conversion?" his mother exclaimed. "What are your kids and my grandkids going to look like, a mongrel?"

"Mom, Kiyoko is beautiful. Your grandchildren will be beautiful."

"Abe, my heart is racing. I may be having a heart attack!"

"Miriam, sit down and take some deep breaths," Moishe yelled in the background.

"Abe, how can you do this to your mother?" she moaned. "No one in our family has ever married outside of our religion. And now you are marrying an idol worshipper. I knew this move to the *fercockta* (screwed-up) Hawaiian Islands was a mistake."

His father came on the line. "Listen, Abe, your mother is not well. We may have to take her to the hospital if her heart doesn't stop racing. We will call you tomorrow when she's feeling better and if she is not having a heart attack, God forbid."

Abe immediately called Adam in a semi-panicked state.

"Adam, I think they would have taken it better if I told them I was gay. At least they wouldn't have to worry about how their grandkids would look." He tugged at his hair. "They were railing about me marrying an idol worshipper."

"What did you expect them to do?" Bombastic replied

dryly. "Plant a tree in Israel or something? Of course, they are going to go meshuga." His voice softened. "Hey, boychik, you are forty years old. You deserve to be happy. The Torah requires it."

Adam paused for breath. "Don't end up like me in a miserable arranged marriage with a woman who despises you. I was actually considering hiring a food taster since her meals were so lousy, I wouldn't be able to tell if she poisoned me or it was just an average meal."

KIYOKO'S FATHER and her mother, Hatsuko, noticed that she was spending lots of time with Abe and that it was more than just business. Hatsuko, who was Japanese and not Okinawan, let her daughter know in no uncertain terms that she did not approve of the relationship.

"Kiyoko, I hope you are not getting serious with this man. No one in our family history has ever married a *haole gaijin*, not to mention a Jewish man. They are a very strange race of gaijins. They wear these little Yamahas on their heads, and all they think about is money."

Kiyoko kept calm. "Mom, they're called yarmulkes, which is the way they show their respect for God, and they are required to give money to charity. Abe is a very kind and generous man."

"Kiyoko, think about if you marry this man what your children would look like — maybe with a big nose."

"Mom, Jewish people are the most educated and most successful group amongst the white people."

"I don't care!" Hatsuko exclaimed. "For generations in our family, we have never intermarried, and you should have enough respect for your ancestors not to do so either!"

She felt her temper rising and carefully reined it in. "Mom, you intermarried with an Okinawan. As you know, Okinawans were mixed in with Chinese and even Portuguese. Their sailors would trade with Okinawa since foreigners were not allowed in Japan for centuries. Many had children with Okinawan women, which is not talked about, but it is a fact."

Kiyoko gathered her courage. "Well, I might as well announce this right now since we are on the subject. Abe and I have decided to marry and that I would convert to Judaism."

The silence following this statement seemed to last an eternity.

"Kiyoko," her mother replied at last, "I don't believe this! You had a chance to marry the Higa boy from a wonderful family and you threw that away. Now you meet this haole, you say you love him, and you want to marry this man with a big nose and convert to his strange religion?"

"Mother," she replied tartly, "if it wasn't for Mr. Silverberg hiring Oji, we wouldn't have our business. You must admit that if it wasn't for that kind man's help, our family might still be laboring in the pineapple fields!"

"I know, but I still don't like it," her mother muttered. "You will have hapa-haole (half Caucasian) children." A heavy sigh. "What is his family like, have you met them yet?"

"Not yet," Kiyoko admitted, "but Abe and I are going to travel to New York soon to meet them."

Her mother gave a satisfied grunt. "*Then* you will see

what you are marrying into, and what your children will be like!"

Miriam Goldstein, whose full lips, bold nose, and thick mane of tawny hair resembled a heavier-set version of the actress and singer Lainie Kazan, was extremely distressed at the turn her son's life had taken.

She decided to bring up the topic with her mahjong group, which met every Wednesday night at Sadie Schwartz's house. It was a potluck, and everyone brought their specialty dish. Miriam was renowned for her beef brisket, which she announced was her son Abe's favorite.

In the theatrical manner that only a distraught Jewish mother could muster, she flung herself onto the sofa and followed up with, "But my son won't have anyone to make brisket for him! He will be eating *treif* (non-kosher food) made by his Japanese wife!"

Miriam got all the sympathetic "oy veys" that she needed. Sophie Sugarman, who was the ringleader of the mahjong cabal, spoke up. "Miriam, I am not saying that I have a solution here. It's not for me to interfere. But why don't you hire a matchmaker to make a shidduch for your son and steal him away from her?"

Sophie lowered her voice to a stage whisper. "Miriam, these Oriental women learn sexual techniques that drive a man crazy, control his mind, like nobody's business. Men are helpless to resist, hypnotized by their charms. Yellow fever, they call it."

She smiled. "But I might have a solution. My sister Sarah had a similar problem. Her son was engaged to a blonde shiksa, beautiful but dumb as a box of rocks. She found these two women, a mother and daughter who run a high-class matchmaking service called Mazel Tov matchmaking. They charge a lot of money but guarantee success.

"Her son Herby was no prize but was a highly successful divorce lawyer and represented her in her divorce. Sarah took one look at the shiksa with her boobs sticking out in a low-cut dress and knew she had to do something.

"So, she hired this mother and daughter's company to find a Jewish maidel match for her Herby. At the same time, the company hired a private detective to investigate the shiksa's background. They find that she was a stripper at a high-end men's club in Las Vegas and had photos obtained for proof. Her stage name was Bobbi Joy."

Miriam gave a grim nod. "I'm not surprised."

"The detective conjured up some phony correspondence from the strip club claiming that she was accused of fleecing a customer, who was threatening to sue the club, and then sent it to Herby in that he was her attorney." Sophie looked around at the group. "That ended the relationship with the bimbo, but the matchmakers knew that he would be very vulnerable at this stage and sprung a trap on poor Herby, a schlimazel if there ever was one."

"They found a Jewish maidel. Attractive but no raving beauty. Had her briefed by Freda, the owner of the matchmaking company who is a shrink, and his mother, Sarah, about his interests and what he liked and then got her invited to a wedding that Herby was attending, had her seated next to him at the dinner table. She reeled him in like a codfish. It cost Sarah twenty-five grand up front and another fifty grand when they got married, but well worth it. She never let on to him what happened. "

"Do you think Mazel Tov matchmakers could do the same for my Abe?" Miriam wondered.

Sophie Sugarman nodded emphatically. "Why not? What do you have to lose?"

"I estimate between fifty to a hundred grand."

The other women all shrugged and nodded.

"Well worth it to have Jewish grandkids," Sadie said.

CHAPTER 7
MAZEL TOV MATCHMAKERS

Miriam Goldstein set up an appointment with Dr. Freda Schwartz, PhD. and her daughter Loni Schwartz, who could have been a finalist in a Joan Rivers Botox competition, at their posh Upper East Side offices in Manhattan.

The waiting room was adorned with tasteful artwork with comfortable leather chairs, and soft music played, setting the scene of a high-class shrink's office, which Dr. Freda was for thirty years before she decided that rather than charge $200 to listen to a neurotic Jewish woman whine for an hour about her asshole husband, she could charge $25k upfront to see them once every couple weeks and have her neurotic daughter hold their hand, take their phone calls, and kiss their ass, under the assumption that neurotics connect best with other neurotics. Her daughter — the veteran of three marriages to a variety of losers, cads, and druggies — would be an expert in vetting the herd of prospects. Loni had a sixth sense that ferreted out losers for everyone but herself.

Also on retainer for the company was private investigator Guido Capezi, a former New York City detective who did due diligence and investigations, sometimes using available public databases and sometimes the not-so-kosher network of "on da job" police officers and various sources of information on marriage prospects. Guido dug into their financial assets, backgrounds, habits, drug use, and any perversions that might become a problem. Loni Schwartz was also the occasional "gumad" (mistress) of Guido Capezi.

The ex-cop also did background investigations on the assets of prospective clients like Miriam Goldstein, much like the plumber checking out the car in the driveway to determine how much they could charge/gouge the client.

"Doc," he'd reported, "Miriam Goldstein is loaded, old Diamond District gelt, connections in Haifa, platinum level at least."

Miriam was impressed with the décor of Dr. Schwartz's office, giving her the impression of plush elegance and class. *Yes,* she thought, *this is the company that can find my Abie an appropriate wife who can bear proper Yiddishkeit grandchildren who would become doctors and lawyers and maybe take over the business.*

Miriam was dreaming about her mythical family-to-be when Dr. Freda greeted her in the waiting room.

"Miriam, may I call you that? It is a pleasure to meet you. From the information that you provided to my daughter Loni, you have a very unusual situation. Let us talk about it. I think we can help."

Miriam rose. "Doctor, my son has lost his mind. He sold his business that has been in the family for generations. He decides to buy a business halfway around the world in Hawaii, where there are almost no Jews, and falls in love with some Japanese seductress who no doubt seduced my Abie with Oriental sexual charms. He is madly in love with her. What can I do?"

Dr. Freda was calculating how much it would cost to pay off the equity loan on the house that she had to take out to pay off her princess daughter's credit card bills after her last divorce and little three-month trip to Europe to "heal her heart" with some Italian gigolo who took her for an expensive ride.

"Miriam, this is a very difficult task that you have given us, but not like we haven't seen this before. We recently successfully broke up a potentially disastrous engagement between a prominent attorney and a stripper from Las Vegas and facilitated a wonderful Jewish girl for him to marry, a storybook ending."

"I know all about it, Baruch Hashem, you can do the same for my Abie. But doctor, above all, you cannot breathe a word of this to anyone, not even my husband, because if this gets back to Abie that I am involved in this mishigas, he will never speak to me again, I am sure."

"Miriam, you have my word, and my company's reputation for privacy and discretion is at stake."

Abe's mother felt a surge of relief. Perhaps this mess could be fixed after all.

"First we are going to have to break up this relationship," Dr. Freda said firmly, "get him vulnerable on the rebound, so to speak, and then set him up with a woman who fits his needs. Of course, we need to be briefed about him, what buttons to push to lure him in. Sometimes this is not a pretty business, but this is what it takes to get what you want, a Jewish family, and frankly this will be costly."

"We have to hire a private detective. We have one that collaborates with us. He's very good. He has a worldwide network that can hopefully dig up some dirt on this girl and her family and get the information to your son in a not-so-obvious manner so as not to have him suspect the source of the info."

She crossed her legs and smiled. "In a situation like this, where the man is not interested in a shidduch and is essentially hostile to our actions, it is exceedingly difficult at best, but if anyone can do this, we can. We ask for a $25,000 retainer upfront and will bill services from there on a project-completion basis. No guarantees here. We get paid if we find a match or not, obviously a significant bonus for a marriage."

Miriam's gaze narrowed. "So, if we go through all of this and my Abie does not bite, I still pay you."

Dr. Freda eyed her placidly. "Yes, but we are the only company who would take a client like you on, and since we have a track record of success in these kinds of circumstances, you have a real shot at getting what you want."

Now for the clincher, thought Freda." Isn't it worth it that you will look back fifteen years from now at your grandson's bar mitzvah and know you made the right choice?"

A fervent nod. "Yes, yes, you are right doctor, I am in. Let's try. Give me a chance to attend my grandson's bar mitzvah."

That settled, Dr. Freda got straight to business. "Miriam, tell me about your son. You have to be honest with me. I know he's wonderful. I can tell from his mother that he is a mensch, but I have to know his fragilities. What kind of man is he? Orthodox, keeps kosher, very moral, or occasionally strays, so to speak? Not trying to be negative, but I have to know what motivates him, and would he be influenced by negative info, and if so, what kind of info would do that?"

"Doctor, if there was something involving a moral issue

that would do it, I know my Abie. He's a mensch like no other. Also, besides breaking him up with this woman, we must set him up with an alternative, a woman that he would want to marry."

"We have a worldwide network of contacts in the US, Europe, Tel Aviv, and even South Africa. This is the most important choice in your son's life, the choice of a partner is highly individualized and specific to your son. I am a trained psychologist and have spent thirty years dealing with relationship issues and am uniquely qualified to assist you along with my staff."

"I submit that we are the best at what we do in selecting a lifelong match, and I am confident that we will have a positive result that will satisfy you and your family's future." She patted Miriam's hand. "I will have my daughter Loni set up an appointment with you to go over every detail in your son's life and personality to begin to start the process of rescuing him from making a terrible mistake."

Miriam wrote Freda a $25,000 check and left the office buoyed that this woman could be the answer to all her problems. She would have to hide the payment from her husband Moishe, but since he never looked at the books, it shouldn't be a problem.

After the meeting, Dr. Freda and her daughter Loni got together in the office and talked about strategy.

"First, I want you to schmooze Miriam to death, make her feel that we dwell on her every concern and are on top of everything. Then I want you to go into her Abie's background — everything — going back to his childhood, bedwetting, even masturbation, and especially old girlfriends. If he doesn't have ex-girlfriends, maybe he is gay. If he had them, who were they? What did they look like?

Photos would be great. Why did they break up? Also delve into his interests. Find out how religious and observant he is and get the name of the Japanese girl from her and any other identifying info that we need to give to Guido."

She pinned her daughter with a hard stare. "Loni, this is a big fish. Do not screw this up. This will be a gold mine if we can pull it off. We can pay off your little fling with your Italian friend who got into your bank account and borrowed $100,000 that he promised he would give back."

Loni scowled. "I knew you would bring that up. I got it. I'll set up an appointment right away."

Guido was sitting in the waiting room, and Loni went to bring him into the office.

"Guido, sit down. Do you want coffee or something? Loni will make it for you."

He shook his head. "Thanks, Doc, I'm fine."

"Okay, Guido, tell me you have good PI contacts in Hawaii."

"Well, Doc, I don't have Dog, the Bounty Hunter," he quipped. "Wouldn't want that idiot anyway. But I've got a local guy, a former cop who got jammed up and left the force. Haven't worked with him for a while, but when he did a small job for me, he got the job done reliably and on time, which is unusual for Hawaii." He leaned forward. "What do you want me to do, get some dirt on this Jap broad, then surreptitiously have the target get forwarded the info? The same routine as the last time?"

"Yes, absolutely."

"From my preliminary checks on what you gave me, it looks like she's from an established Japanese family in the diamond business. It sounds like the gal is straight." Guido shrugged his heavy shoulders. "Hey, maybe there's an abortion in the mix or something. Who knows?"

Freda shot him a steely look. "Get creative if you have to, Guido. Your budget is 5K. If you have to go higher than that, you better have her dressing in male drag."

KIMO ORNELLAS HAD BEEN a PI since he left the Honolulu police department five years ago, when his family was identified as being involved in a gambling operation in Chinatown. Kimo was suspected of providing information to the gambling ring about police activity in the area and was asked to resign. By resigning and not being fired, he was eligible to become a licensed PI in the state.

"Hey Kimo, I got a job for you, pal," Guido said on the phone.

"Braddah, talk to me. What you got me doing?"

"I want you to try to dig up some dirt on this broad that is engaged to my client's son. My client wants to break it up really badly. Her name is Kiyoko Arakaki. She's from an Okinawan-Japanese family that owned a diamond engagement ring business in Honolulu. I think it is now called Shaloha Gems. I'll send you the details."

"I heard of dem. Dey advertise on TV all da time here."

"Kimo, keep your budget below two grand. If you come up with something, we can possibly raise it."

"Roger that, brah."

AFTER A LENGTHY MEETING WITH MIRIAM, in which Loni got way too much information on Abie, she returned to the Mazel Tov office and sat down with her mother to strategize some ideas for a match for Abe Goldstein.

"He's kind of a rebellious mama's boy," she reported, glancing at her notes, "lived at home till he was twenty-five, then moved in with a roommate from college, Yeshiva University. Spent a year in Israel while in college and hooked up with a beautiful Israeli woman. Fell in love with her, and she led him on to think they were going to get married. Miriam was strewing flowers in her path, he got her a three-carat engagement ring, and to make a long story short, she later dumped him for some macho Israeli commando-type and kept the ring. He followed her like a puppy dog, and she shit all over him."

"According to Miriam, she was very sexy but a 'bitch on wheels.' I got a photo of her from Miriam."

Freda looked at the photo depicting a dark Sephardic-type of woman, Moroccan or Yemenite background, slim and big-breasted, with long black hair.

"She made quite a score on the ring," Loni said with a touch of admiration, "worth about fifty grand, and Abe was crushed. He goes back and forth to Israel for business and has lots of relatives in the diamond business in Haifa. Rumor has it that his relatives there tried to make a shidduch for him, but he would not go for it."

Dr. Freda skimmed her list of women, looking for an appropriate match.

"We need a nurturing type, somewhat like his Yiddishe momma, but not a nagging yenta. I will send this photo out to our contacts in New York, Los Angeles, Tel Aviv, London, and South Africa to see if they have anyone on their register that looks similar. Men like a certain style of women. There are some they *schtup* and some they marry. Let's see if we can dangle the right bait to attract him for the *schtup* and reel him in for the marriage."

"First, we have to break it up," Loni pointed out. "Guido has to pull a rabbit out of his hat."

GUIDO CONTACTED Kimo a couple times a week, but no info was forthcoming. And Guido was getting pressured by Dr. Freda.

"Kimo, talk to me, pal. You got to come up with something. My client is all over me like a cheap suit."

"Hey Brah, I used all my connections on dis, da wahine is straight as dey come, had a boyfriend, Okinawan kid, son of her Fadda's friend, broke up. She spends her time working at the family store and taking care of her father and grandfather. Even got her medical records from where you do not want to know, dis kid is clean, notting dere."

"Damn Kimo, that is what I was afraid of, a Japanese Goldilocks. Hey, get creative. Maybe we can get proof that she had a secret life as a stripper or hooking on the side or something?"

"Hey, Guido, dat's a stretch. How am I gonna do dat?"

"Ok, how's this? Go to a local strip club. Find a Japanese girl who looks like our gal and get a nude pic of her. We Photoshop it with her face and get the picture to the client's son surreptitiously."

"Surrup . . . what?"

"Masking the origin of the info, which comes from another source that he trusts, who believes it is righteous, and is reluctant to show it to him but feels compelled to do so."

"Got it, but dats a lowdown ting."

Kimo sounded like he was shaking his head in disgust.

"What if I talk to my client and see if we can add

another grand to your fee?" Guido suggested. "But this has got to work, or we are screwed."

"Make it two grand, and we are good."

"You get the extra grand if the scheme works, Kimo."

BACK AT THE Mazel Tov office, Dr. Freda and Loni went into overtime scanning their databases worldwide for women that fit the description of the Israeli vixen that took Abe to the cleaners. Dr. Freda pulled out all stops doing an executive-level search with all her worldwide contacts, with her daughter Loni doing follow-ups on all the prospects.

"Loni, sweetheart, what do you have for me?"

"Got an interesting prospect from a matchmaker based in Cape Town, South Africa. The girl they have in mind is tall, thin, with dark eyes and long black hair. And get this, she's the daughter of an Orthodox wholesale diamond dealer."

Loni showed her mother a picture. "Look at this photo, she is college-educated in England, wears glasses, looks attractive, she was a musician and played the flute, she must be bright, the question is why is she not remarried yet?"

"Well, she has been divorced and has a young girl. Hopefully, that won't be a problem."

Loni added with a smirk, "Since she plays the flute, she might have a particular talent that might hook our Abie."

"Nice thought, Loni. You always have that unique cerebral perspective on relationships."

"I would bet on it, momala."

◈

Kimo spent the next few nights at Rockza, a famous strip club in Honolulu. The girls at Rockza were known to be the best-looking on the islands. Kimo bought some drinks for "Aiko," a Korean Japanese stripper who had a similar build to Kiyoko without the boob job common amongst Asian strippers.

"Will you buy me some champagne, handsome?"

"Sista, I no can buy you champagne, but I can pay you for someting."

"Yeah, well, I don't turn tricks." She eyed him warily. "What are you working, Vice? You don't look familiar to me."

"No tricks. I will buy you a drink and have a friend that wants to buy some special photos of you for his collection."

A plucked brow lifted. "How special do you want these photos?"

"Da more special da betta. Bring some photos wit you tomorrow night, and I'll let you know if I want dem and how much I pay for dem."

"You got it, handsome. I'll be here about 7:00 p.m. and work till 2:00 a.m."

"See you tomorrow."

Kimo did some checking on Aiko with his pals on HPD Vice and found out that she did make some money on the side doing "adult" films and had a drug dealer boyfriend who was suspected of dealing "shabu" crystal meth.

Kimo showed up at Rockza at seven sharp the next night and watched Aiko's performance — and she got his full attention. He waited in a booth until after her performance. Then she put on an almost see-through gown and came over to the booth.

"Hey, handsome, I got what you wanted."

"Okay, let's see."

Aiko showed some nude shots of herself, leaving nothing to the imagination. "I'll give three of these shots to you for $250. Now, if you want some really hot video stuff, it will cost you $500."

Kimo realized that he would not be able to Photoshop the videos, so he wasn't interested in them.

"I'll take the three photos and give you a hundred bucks for 'em."

"A hundred fifty."

"A hundred twenty-five."

"Sold."

Kimo sent the photos back to Guido via overnight mail, along with photographs of Kiyoko obtained through the diamond businesses photographer.

"Good work, Kimo. Now I'll have my Photoshop wizard work his magic and see what he can create."

Miriam met Dr. Freda at the Mazel Tov office, and they had afternoon tea together in Freda's private office with an impressive view of the East River.

"Miriam, I've got good news for you. We have located a Jewish girl from South Africa who might fit the bill for your son."

"Tell me more."

"She is thirty-one years old, the daughter of an Orthodox diamond dealer, educated in London, and was a professional musician before she moved back to South

Africa. Her parents paid for a shidduch through a match-maker in Tel Aviv, but nothing clicked for her.

"I must tell you that she is divorced with a young eight-year-old daughter and currently lives with her father and mother in Cape Town. Here is her photo, slim and pretty."

Miriam was hopeful. "Yes, she is pretty, she is slim the way my Abie likes them, is she Orthodox?"

"I don't know, but her parents are. They keep kosher, so she must. Okay, Miriam, I'm gathering she meets with your approval. So now we have to do the setup for the meet and have it look accidental. At the same time, we are going to spring a surprise on Abie that will get him to question his faith in this girl's morality and whether he wants to go through with this marriage. At that point, enter Shoshanna from South Africa, an exotic dark-haired beauty to reel him in. It's our best shot."

Miriam bit her lip. "Doctor, how are we going break him up with the Japanese girl? How do you plan to do that?"

"You don't want to know, but this is the only chance we have to break this up. You have to trust my years of experience in these matters. Miriam, now you have to help me with this. Do you have an event that he has to attend?"

"As a matter of fact, I do. We have a bar mitzvah coming up in a couple of weeks for one of my nephews' kids. It will be held in the Catskills."

"Great, make sure he is committed to going. Also, get his business partner invited to the event. I will arrange for Shoshanna to come in from South Africa, and you need to talk to your niece about getting her invited, too. Give her some B.S. story that she is a distant relative that you found online and that she is coming to the states, knows no one here, and it would be a mitzvah if you could invite her to the Bar Mitzvah. Also, ask if she can sit at the table next to Abe. This is essential."

Miriam nodded. "Dr. Freda, my relative owes me some favors. I will call in the favor on this one. I will go to shul and give to charity to do a mitzvah and will pray this will happen."

KIMO RECEIVED the photoshopped pictures from Guido via overnight mail. The Photoshop guy did a great job, undetectable except to experts that it was altered. Three photos of a nude Asian girl in various seductive poses with nothing left to the imagination. The woman appeared to be in her early or mid-twenties, a younger version of Kiyoko.

On Guido's instructions, a few weeks later, just prior to Abe and Adam departing for New York to attend the bar mitzvah, Kimo sent the photos to Adam Buskin with a written note.

"I just want to let you know that Kiyoko is not who your business partner thinks she is. However, as his best friend, I just want to let you know. So, you should watch out for him."

The letter was postmarked the day before from Honolulu. Adam was in shock at what he saw. He was very upset and conflicted as to what to do. This would devastate Abe; he was head over heels in love with Kiyoko. *I cannot do this to him,* he thought miserably. *It would destroy him.*

Adam immediately put in a call to the rabbi to ask him what to do and left a message on his voicemail indicating that he needed to speak to him about an important matter.

But the rabbi was out of town and did not get back to him before he left with Abe for New York.

THE BAR MITZVAH was held at Kirshner's Hotel in the Catskill Mountains, also known as the Jewish Alps.

It was a high-end affair with an orthodox rabbi from the neighborhood where the young bar mitzvah boy Mendel lived. Mendel gave the required "today I am a man" speech, and every relative was called up to the dais to light a candle and give an envelope to the young man.

A klezmer band was playing for the party afterward, with a kosher buffet spread that could feed the IDF for a week. An open bar was available, and Adam was on his third scotch when he received a call from Rabbi Shmuley in Honolulu.

Adam explained his dilemma to the rabbi without giving him specific details and told him that he was conflicted as to what to do.

"Adam, as you know, idle gossip is forbidden in the Torah, but this is not idle gossip. You seem to be convinced that this is verifiable, so given that he is your best friend, I think you should tell him."

Adam went back to the table that was assigned to him and Abe and found Abe engrossed in a conversation with an attractive woman with a South African accent.

"Adam, this is Shoshanna," he said. "Her father is a diamond dealer in Cape Town. My mother connected with her through family tree DNA and found that she is a distant relative of ours. She told my mother that she was going to be in New York on business, so my mother had her invited to the bar mitzvah. She is a musician by training and played for the London Symphony for a few years until she moved back to South Africa. Adam, you were a musician in your younger days, were you not?"

"Yes, I was a violinist and played while I attended Yeshiva. At one point, I realized that I would never be mistaken for Itzhak Perlman or Jascha Heifetz, so I decided to go into accounting." He smiled politely, though his stomach was roiling. Adam looked as uncomfortable as a monk at a strip club. "Abe, can I have a word with you for a moment at the bar?"

Abe and Adam walked to the bar, and Adam ordered his fourth scotch to build up his courage.

"Abe, I did not want to give you this information, but after talking to the rabbi, I felt I must. I got a letter before I left with some photos that I want you to look at."

Adam pulled the photos out of his pocket and showed them to Abe.

It was like someone had punched Abe in the stomach, and he doubled over in pain.

"No, Adam, it can't be, it can't be true, Kiyoko would never pose for photos like this, who sent these to you, do you have any idea?"

"Abe, I don't know. I'm guessing her ex-boyfriend."

He raised a shaking hand to his forehead. "Leave me alone, please, Adam. I have to think about this. My whole life is upside down."

Adam went back to the table and sat next to Shoshanna. Within minutes, Shoshanna and Adam became engrossed in conversation about life and music and every-thing. There was an unmistakable chemistry between them.

About thirty minutes later, Abe came back to the table and asked to speak to Adam privately.

"I am convinced that these photos are not of Kiyoko," he whispered, relief in his eyes.

"Really, how do you know?"

"This woman has a butterfly tattoo above her *tuchas* (rear end) which Kiyoko does not have."

Adam arched a brow. "I am being indelicate to ask, but how do you know she doesn't have one?"

"Because remember when we went paddling on the outrigger canoe that time in Waikiki? I was seated right behind her and she was wearing a bikini. Well, I would have noticed that tattoo and she did not have one!" He stabbed a finger for emphasis.

Adam nodded. "Yes, you're right! I remember you were right behind her." He frowned. "Could this have been Photoshopped with Kiyoko's face inserted?"

The men shared a long look. "I don't know," Abe replied, "but I will bring this to an expert that does Photoshop for commercials and see what he says." He looked angry and appalled. "Who could do this?"

"Could be the ex-boyfriend, this Higa guy, but I have somebody else in mind who would benefit."

"Yup, Kenji Ono. What a dirtbag!"

Adam glanced across the hotel ballroom. "Abe, by the way, I really like that South African girl who is at our table. I would like to change seats with you if you don't mind."

"Sure, Adam." He patted his back. "Good luck, pal."

Miriam dropped by the table and said hello, noticing that Abe had changed seats with Adam and that Adam was making goo-goo eyes with the South African girl seated next to him.

Miriam became visibly upset.

"Ma, what's wrong? Are you okay?"

"Yes, yes," she muttered distractedly, "it must be something I ate."

As they both watched, Adam lead Shoshanna out to the dance floor.

"Hey, ma, I think Adam is in love. It was great that you invited her to the bar mitzvah! He has been very depressed after his divorce, and this really picked him up." He patted his mother's hand. "It was a mitzvah that you invited her."

"Yes, Abe," she said sourly, "a real mitzvah."

Abe later confirmed through his photographer friend that the photos were altered. His friend advised that this was done by a professional and not some amateur on his home computer. Abe called Adam while still in New York and told him the news.

"Baruch Hashem, you were right. It was a dirty trick by that bastard, Ono."

"Who else could it be besides him or the ex-boyfriend?"

"We may never know but thank god we figured it out."

"Abe, by the way, I'm going to stay in New York for a week or so. I am going to spend some time with Shoshanna before she goes back to South Africa."

"Great, what luck that my mother invited her! It was meant to be."

MIRIAM SET up a meeting with Dr. Freda at the Mazel Tov office that next Monday. Dr. Freda and Loni were excited to hear how it went.

"Tell me, Miriam, what happened? You don't look happy."

"*Happy*, you ask me if I am *happy*? I just spent $25,000

to set up a match for my son, and you charged me expenses over $15,000 for the girl's trip to the states and for the private investigator to make a match with my son's accountant, and you ask me if I am *happy*?"

She gave a forceful exhale through her nose. "I, of course, cannot ask him what happened for fear he would know I was involved and would never speak to me again, but obviously, he figured it out and did not buy whatever you did.

"I thought you people were professionals, the best! You made the perfect match all right for Adam Buskin, which cost me over $40,000. Maybe you can collect the balance for the match from him?"

Miriam stormed out of the office, murmuring one last word: "Goniffs!"

Thieves.

Dr. Freda turned to Loni. "So, what's with Shoshanna? What does she say?" Her lips pursed in thought. "Well, if this leads to marriage, we get paid by her family, which is nice."

"She said she found her soulmate in Adam, and he is apparently crazy over her," Loni reported. "They shacked up for a few days in the Catskills and are making plans already. He was on the rebound from an ugly divorce and was ripe for the taking."

"And she was a flute player," Dr. Freda replied dryly. "Obviously, a very good one."

CHAPTER 8
KIYOKO MEETS THE MISHUGA MISHPUCHA (CRAZY JEWISH FAMILY)

Abe called his mother and said he wanted to have Kiyoko come with him to New York City to meet the family.

"Ma, I'd like her to meet the mishpucha (family) and see what she's getting into. Give her a chance to back out."

The eruption was immediate. "Abe, my god, what will I feed her? What will she eat?"

"Ma, she only eats raw fish, so go to the City Island bait and tackle shop and buy a few pounds of raw bait. She and her brother, who is coming with her, will eat that with seaweed and rice."

"Are you serious, Abe?" Miriam's voice climbed another octave. "I can't buy treif!"

Abe covered the phone to muffle his laughter. "Just kidding, ma. She and her brother will eat everything — with the possible exception of your lead matzo balls. I will put them up at the local Hilton on Sheepshead Bay and give them a tour of Coney Island, all the places where I grew up, although I might have to rent a bulletproof vest."

The next phone call after Abe hung up was to Miriam's girlfriend.

"Sophie, what am I going to do?" she wailed. "My son is bringing this Oriental seductress back to New York to meet the family. What am I going to do?"

Sophie told Miriam, "Listen, have a family circle meeting, better yet at the Chanukah party, invite the most obnoxious, most meshuga relatives that you can find, and make it look like the bar scene in the movie *Star Wars*. It will scare the hell out of her. One look at that gene pool will have her on the next plane to Honolulu."

Freda, Miriam, and Sophie had a strategy session at the Mazel Tov matchmaker's office, after Miriam relented in desperation and returned for their advice.

"We can invite Uncle Milty who is a walking fart machine. We can't light a match around Milty or the room will explode. He erupts like the volcano in Hawaii, hopefully without any lava flow, if you know what I mean."

"How about Cousin Shmuel with the long beard? After every meal, he likes to show off what he ate by leaving it on his beard."

"Remember Schmuel's lovely wife Hannah, a yenta (non-stop talker) like you wouldn't believe."

"How about the Rabbi Mendel who has breath like a blowtorch? He could curl your hair, and his fat wife, Sadie. We have to supersize the toilet seat when she visits."

"Can't forget my cousin Pearl. We can sit her next to the Japanese girl, and after ten minutes of her kvetching (complaining) and telling her about her bowel movements, she would drive Dr. Ruth to drink."

ABE AND ADAM arrived a few days earlier prior to Kiyoko and her brother Yoshi's arrival at JFK Airport. Abe drove his family's Lexus SUV to pick them up. He brought some warm coats for Kiyoko and her brother and drove them to the Hilton Hotel in Sheepshead Bay, Brooklyn.

Driving on New York freeways had Kiyoko and Yoshi terrified with the amount of traffic and the horns honking. Driving into Sheepshead Bay, the traffic died down to a crawl, and a taxi driver in a yellow cab shouted at Abe after they maneuvered for a lane, "Hey, fuck you, pal!" waving a one finger salute at the car.

"Welcome to New York, Kiyoko," Abe said with a straight face. "That's the traditional greeting to all new visitors."

Kiyoko looked like she was in shock. "Abe, does everyone act like that here?"

"Not everyone," Adam answered," but you can count on most New York cab drivers to make the gesture at least once a day."

Yoshi remarked that, "If dat guy did dat in Hawaii to a Hawaiian, Samoan, or Tongan, dey would have picked him up wit a sponge, brah."

The next day Abe and Adam met Kiyoko at the hotel for breakfast. Kiyoko and Yoshi had eggs, and Yoshi had some pork rolls with the eggs. Adam and Abe just had coffee, saving their appetite for a later lunch at Lundy's restaurant.

Yoshi said, "Hey, sorry, I got to have my pork or bacon with my eggs. Dis pork roll is ono. Hope you guys don't mind."

Adam joked, "No, we don't mind Yoshi, but just don't ask for pork roll at Miriam's house. It might elicit an 'Oy vey'."

Abe added, "A mega *oy vey*."

Kiyoko and her brother complained about the air quality, and their eyes were constantly watering. They were coughing and sneezing.

"Ah," Adam said, waving a hand, "it's just because you're not used to breathing air you can see."

Abe had his driver Tyrone pick them up at the hotel and drive them to Coney Island for a tour. Tyrone was a large Black man with a shaved head and acted as Abe's driver and bodyguard. The Coney Island area of Brooklyn was near the Brighton Beach district, which was the center of Russians and Russian Jews, with a major element of Russian organized crime. Signs on shops were in Yiddish and the Russian Cyrillic alphabet. Stores sold pierogis and borscht, hawkers approached the group on the boardwalk, but one look from Tyrone and they backed off.

As Kiyoko, Yoshi, Abe, and Adam were strolling on the boardwalk, Abe pointed out the famous Coney Island parachute jump that had long since closed but was a remnant of an age gone by until vicious plaintiffs' lawyers filed lawsuits at the drop of a hat. That liability closed down the landmark site.

Since it was summer, the beach was crowded with throngs of people on blankets, chairs and lounges with huge canvas umbrellas that would become a flying spear in a windstorm. They came from every nationality, the black people with tons of bling jewelry, Italians wearing crosses and hot pepper pendants, Puerto Ricans wearing crosses, and Jews wearing Star of David pendants.

Yoshi wondered whether any of these people ever went into the ocean since a pound or two of gold might sink them if they got by the shore break. At the end of the day, recluses with metal detectors and headphones would usually produce a chain or two, maybe even a ring for their efforts.

Vendors selling knishes or ice cream screamed at ten decibels, causing the kids on the beach to nudge their parents into buying something, even if they were not hungry.

"Abe, I told you that we could do a side gig in Honolulu selling taro knishes and bagels, get a food truck with new fusion cuisine — Jew Bu. A Jewish-Buddhist vegan menu, rice matzo ball soup."

"Adam, lets stick with the jewelry store for now, bubala."

"Yoshi, do you think you could handle being a lifeguard here? I hear there are openings."

"Brah, da wave action here is not a problem, kinda cold water, but I tink I would need a translator, and maybe a waterproof bulletproof vest."

After the stroll on the boardwalk in Coney Island, they all headed back to the hotel, where they dropped off Kiyoko and Yoshi to freshen up in their rooms. Adam and Abe drove back to Long Island to get ready to take them to dinner at his parents' home in Long Island. On the drive, Abe said he feared his mother might be scheming to sabotage the engagement.

Adam came out with it directly. "Abe, I know your mother. Correct me if I'm wrong: she wants you to marry Kiyoko likes she wants breast cancer."

He sighed. "Adam, she must have some kind of meshuga plan in mind. Use your yiddisha kup (Jewish brain) to figure it out what she's planning. Doesn't your mother play mahjong once in a while with my mother's friends? That's where their plot will be hatched."

Abe picked up Yoshi and Kiyoko and drove them to the

family home, located in a gated community in Long Island. Miriam and Moishe greeted them at the front door, with Miriam sporting her best dress, her most expensive jewelry, and an N95 mask.

"Dahling," she purred, "you have to wear a mask when you come in. Moishe here is in his eighties, he gets a Covid he is a goner. Here, take these masks please." She thrust out a hand. "Kiko, you look so pretty, like a China doll. I must have seen the movie *Sayonara* ten times. I was bawling at the end when Red Buttons and the Japanese girl Katsumi committed suicide."

Abe winced. "Ma, her name is Kiyoko, and I don't think she was even born when that movie was playing."

Miriam awkwardly attempted to hug Kiyoko. Kiyoko was taken aback by the large Jewish mama with huge gold earrings crushing her.

"And you must be her brother, what did you say your name was?"

"My name is Yoshi, Mrs. Goldstein."

"Yoshi sounds like Yoni, which is a Hebrew name." She might have smiled, though it was hard to tell behind the mask. "Nice to meet you." Miriam stepped back and drew them all inside. "Sit down, sit down, eat, eat. Kiko, I mean Kiyoko, you look too skinny! We got gefilte fish, kugel, brisket of beef, matzo ball soup. You will love it."

Yoshi looked at Abe and whispered, "Hey brah, what is gefilte fish?"

"Yoshi, you don't want to know, just put hot horse-radish on it and you won't taste a thing."

Yoshi and Kiyoko were seated at the end of the table, both coughing and blowing their noses.

"What's wrong mit dem?" Moishe asked.

"Pop, they can't handle the pollution around here.

They're used to clean air and water in Hawaii."

Yoshi said, "Yeah, unless Madame Pele gets pissed and we hear from her, den da vog comes ova and it's not good."

Miriam asked him, "Yoni, I mean Yoshi, who is Madame Pele, some kind of Hawaiian princess?"

"No, she's da goddess of the volcano, da Hawaiians believe in her big time."

"They believe in a pagan goddess in the mountain," Miriam repeated. "Do you believe in her?"

"I don't dismiss anything; strange things happen ova dere."

Her eyes gleamed with malice. "Kiyoko, dear, do you believe that, too?"

Kiyoko seemed to choose her words with care. "Mrs. Goldstein, in Shinto Buddhism, the Japanese believe that innate objects possess a spirit."

Miriam whispered to Moishe, "I told you we're going to get an idol worshipper for a daughter-in-law, kina *hora* (the evil eye)." She turned back to her future daughter-in-law. "Kiyoko, you are going to maintain a Jewish household, aren't you?"

Abe jumped in on the cross-examination. "Ma, we already went over this, Kiyoko is studying under Rabbi Shmuley and is in the process of converting, you don't have to give her the third degree."

Kiyoko shot him a grateful look and gripped his hand under the table.

After dinner, as Abe, Kiyoko and Yoshi departed, Miriam gave a less than passionate "air kiss" to Kiyoko.

"Dahling, we are going to see you and your brother on Friday night for the first night of Chanukah, aren't we?"

Kiyoko nodded and said, "Oh, yes."

After they left, Miriam quipped, "Moishe, the girl and her brother were sneezing and coughing, maybe she has some kind of Asian Covid?"

THE NEXT DAY, Abe and Adam drove Kiyoko and Yoshi to the New Jersey Meadowlands to watch the New York Jets play the New England Patriots. Adam got them seats in a friend's corporate box. The stadium was filled, the parking lot was jammed, and even with VIP parking it took forty-five minutes to get out of the parking lot.

"Brah, I thought that we had traffic in Honolulu, but dis is crazy."

"Yoshi, you ain't seen nothing yet," said Adam. "An average commute on the Long Island Expressway during rush hour is a two-hour-plus root canal."

Adam called Abe later that night and told him what he had heard from his mother at the latest mahjong strategy session.

"Abe," he said breathlessly, "they are going to showcase the most obnoxious relatives and friends at the Chanukah party that your mother has to scare Kiyoko off from marrying into this meshuga family."

Abe's lips thinned at her diabolical cunning. "Adam, I suspected that something was going on, I can read my mother like a book. My father I'm sure is not involved and would not even be told about the plan."

The next day was the first night of Chanukah. Abe decided it would be wise to prepare Kiyoko and Yoshi about what to expect.

"Kiyoko, Yoshi, we will be going to the Chanukah celebration at the Chabad house tonight. My mother and father are big contributors to Chabad, which mainly depends on donations of the attendees. It's not like a normal community synagogue that has memberships. My family are big machers (important people) at the temple, so we will be seated at the table with the rabbi. Generally, Chabad is welcoming to outsiders, even to non-Jews, but in this case Adam and I will try to buffer you and Yoshi away from some of the crazier members of the congregation."

The group arrived at the Chabad Jewish Center of South Hampton prior to sundown when the holiday begins. There were tables set up with a dais in the front of the room where the Rabbi Mendel, his family, and major contributors (big machers) were seated. Place settings were arranged with Kiyoko next to Miriam and the rabbi.

Before everyone was seated, Abe switched the location of the place settings so that Yoshi and Kiyoko were buffered on either side by Abe and Adam, moving his obnoxious relatives' placards to other tables and replacing them with decent relatives that he had previously called and invited.

When Miriam came to the table, she exclaimed, "Where's Pearl? Where's Uncle Milty, Shmuel, and Hannah?"

"They decided that they wanted to share the pleasure of their company with others," Abe said, "not to just a small group, but to spread their wonderful nachas (joy) around the room."

Miriam caught the sarcasm and responded with a terse, "Of course, of course."

After everyone was seated, the rabbi got up and gave a "L'Chaim" (to life) toast with glasses of schnapps being raised. "L'Chaim!" Everyone cried.

Adam and Abe threw down the schnapps and gave a hearty "L'Chaim." Yoshi and Kiyoko did not drink alcohol but toasted with grape juice instead.

The rabbi got up to speak, trying to get the congregation's attention by hitting his spoon on the glass goblet.

"Today, we commemorate the festival of lights, a miracle that happened more than 2100 years ago when the Israelites won a miraculous military victory over the Hellenic Greeks, culminating with the dedication of the holy temple in Jerusalem and the rekindling of the menorah, which had been desecrated and extinguished by the enemy.

"The Chanukah menorah is a symbol of the triumph of freedom over oppression, of spirit over matter, and of light over darkness. The Chanukah lights remind us that illumination begins at home within oneself and one's family, but also for others in the vicinity. Indeed, the Chanukah lights are expressly meant to illuminate the outside bringing light to those who for some reason still walk in darkness."

While the rabbi was speaking, the crowd continued to talk over him, carrying on conversations amongst each other. Children were running around the room helter-skelter, uncontrolled by their parents.

Kiyoko whispered Abe, "Abe this is so rude, everyone talking while the rabbi is trying to speak, their kids are running around like wild animals."

Adam overheard the conversation and said one word to Abe: "Yiddiluch." *Jews.*

Abe tried to explain. "Kiyoko the Jews are an emotional and creative people. The creative mind usually lacks discipline and is rarely organized, subsequently chaos usually reigns."

As soon as the words came out of Abe's mouth, the

rabbi and his helpers attempted to light the huge menorah with a stepladder. The rabbi's lighter would not work so a zippo lighter was produced. The rabbi teetered on the edge of the stepladder, attempting to reach the wick of the candle, lost his balance, and tumbled off of the ladder, luckily being caught by his helpers.

Miriam was startled. "Oh, my god, maybe he is injured, are you alright, rabbi?"

He raised his hand and waved. "I'm okay, everybody, I'm okay."

A longer stemmed lighter was produced from the kitchen and the rabbi tried it again, but for some reason the wicks would not light, so the kitchen staff brought out two birthday candles, placed one on the menorah dripping wax to make it adhere to the existing larger candle and then the rabbi lit the other birthday candle to light the one on the menorah.

"L'chaim! We now will open up the buffet, please proceed by table."

The Rebbetzin (the rabbi's wife) read off the tables to access the buffet. "Table One, please."

Adam's table was called first to the buffet since that was the donor table.

Kiyoko followed Adam and Abe through the buffet line and got a running description from Adam on the food.

"Kiyoko, watch out for the lead latkes, got to drown 'em in apple sauce but stay close to the bathroom, these pastries are great, so is the kugel noodle dish, there are discount coupons for the Jenny Craig weight loss center at the end of the table."

As Kiyoko and Yoshi moved to the buffet table with the gefilte fish, lox, bagels, cream cheese, raw onions, and smoked whitefish, the majority of the guests also rushed to the same buffet table.

Much like the Secret Service protecting and whisking away a VIP, Abe and Adam quickly maneuvered Kiyoko and Yoshi out of the way from the first wave of the Jewish bonsai charge for the bagels and lox.

"Abe, what are you doing!"

"Kiyoko, I'm saving you from getting trampled by a pack of hungry Jews. Never get between Jews and a lox tray or you will be run over, flattened like a taro pancake."

Adam added, "It's the charge of the lox brigade." He started to solemnly recite: "Half a latke, half a latke, half a latke onward, into the valley of nosh rode the lox brigade . . . Forward the lox brigade, charge for the bagels he said, lox to the left of them, latkes to the right of them, kugel in front of them, which to grab first? They wondered . . ."

"Adam, enough already," barked Abe.

Kiyoko and Yoshi were laughing hysterically.

"Abe, we have a saying in Okinawan' Harahachi bu', meaning only eat until you are 80% full, never overeat, that's why Okinawans live so long"

Adam replied "Kiyoko, I don't there is such a thing as a harahachi bu jew, the jewish version of harahaci bu is a gastric bypass"

Kiyoko laughed "your people are so entertaining, never a dull moment."

He sobered up. "Entertaining? You want entertainment? Here comes Cousin Pearl to say hello."

"Abe-ala," she sang, "I'm so glad you could come back home for Chanukah, I see you brought your girlfriend. Hello dear, my name is Pearl, this is my husband Milty."

Abe and Adam had already worked out a routine to handle the "meshugah mishpocha" (crazy family).

"Pearl, this is Kiyoko and her brother Yoshi, they flew in a few days ago."

"You are so beautiful, Kikko! I just loved the *Flower Drum Song* movie with Nancy Kwan, you look a little like Nancy Kwan."

Kiyoko replied politely, "Pearl, that's a Chinese story. My name is Kiyoko, I'm Okinawan Japanese."

Pearl blathered on. "Oh, I get them all mixed up, you know we always go to a Chinese restaurant on Christmas day when no one else is open. Kosher of course, I just love egg drop soup. Kikko, isn't this the year of the horse or something?"

Abe jumped in. "Thank you, Aunt Pearl, good to see you, happy Chanukah!"

Adam chimed in. "Reminds me of a joke about a Jewish guy and a Chinese guy sitting in a bar. The Jewish guy, Goldberg, hauls off and belts the Chinese guy, Wong, and knocks him to the floor. Wong, all shocked, asks, what was that for? Goldberg says Pearl Harbor. Wong then yells back, You idiot! The Japanese bombed pearl harbor, not the Chinese!

"Wong then slugs Goldberg and knocks him off the bar stool. What was that for? Wong answers, "The Titanic. The Titanic? What the hell are you talking about? Wong replies, Goldberg, Iceberg, what's the difference?"

The young kids were spinning dreidels (tops) on the floor in front of the dais, screaming and yelling. One fat little girl started screaming, "I won, I won, you cheated!"

The boy she was playing with grabbed all of the gold-wrapped chocolate coins called "Chanukah gelt." In an instant, the fat girl grabbed the smaller boy by the hair and wrestled the chocolate coins away from him, breaking his glasses in the process.

Kiyoko could not believe this behavior. "Where are the parents of these kids?" she wondered. "They let them disrupt the whole place?"

Adam told her, "The parents are arguing about politics in the other room. One group backs Bernie Sanders. The other group thinks he's not liberal enough."

Abe glanced around warily. "I think it's time we made our exit before Miriam sends in the heavy artillery."

"You mean the 250-pound rabbi's wife?" Adam asked.

"Yeah, Kiyoko, if she hugs you, she may crush you like a grape, we better get out of here. I'm going to let Miriam know we are leaving." Abe quickly tracked his mother down. "Ma, we have to leave. Kiyoko is not feeling well."

"What? Abe, she hasn't even tasted my delicious cheesecake. She can't leave now!"

He pecked her cheek. "Bye, ma."

Back with the others, he said, "I'll call my mother after the party and tell her that Kiyoko tested positive for Covid on a home test kit. Then tomorrow, I will call her and tell her we had her retested and we all tested negative." He smiled. "That will panic my mother since she bear-hugged Kiyoko and will think she has it and that she spread it around to her obnoxious friends and relatives. *That* should send her a message that I did not appreciate her little scheme."

The next morning Abe called his mother.

"Ma, Kiyoko tested positive for Covid."

"Oh, my god, Abe, I hugged and kissed her, and I hugged and kissed all the guests, I am feeling a little sick, what should I do?"

"I don't know, but you better tell your guests that they may have just hugged Typhoid Mary." He grinned at the phone. "Or should I say, Covid Miriam?"

CHAPTER 9
NOT SO ONO'S DIAMONDS

When Abe got back to Honolulu, he was reluctant to bring up the photo incident to Kiyoko, or to her father or brother. He made some discreet inquiries about Kiyoko's former fiancé, but from everything that he discovered, the guy was a dull, bland type of personality, and it would be out of character for him to try to pull something like this.

Besides, he had been married for five years with two children. It's possible that he held a grudge against Kiyoko, but not likely. Kenji Ono was the most likely suspect, but nothing could be proven.

Shaloha Gems was advertising on the local TV stations using Abe in the commercials wearing his flowered yarmulke, saying, "Shalom, we get our diamonds straight from the diamond center of the world, Tel Aviv, Israel, direct to Honolulu with no middleman."

Then Kiyoko and her father chime in using the "shaka" sign, saying, "We give Aloha and mahalo to every customer local style, it's the best of both worlds. Shalom prices and Aloha service, Shalom & Aloha means Shaloha Gems."

Shaloha Gems had a high-end aspect of their business that was unique to the Hawaiian Islands, with a worldwide network of diamond and gem contacts that no one in the Pacific outside of India could match. Abe personally knew the owner of the pink diamond mine in Western Australia and natural sapphire miners in Sri Lanka, all orthodox Jews. Abe brought in a high-end jewelry designer from Manhattan who, like everyone in NYC, wanted to get the hell out. Those high-end buyers were mainly from China. Adam was even talking about getting into the high-end international jewelry market in Maui, where the wealthy from around the world keep second and third homes. But that was down the line.

Kenji Ono's business sales were slowly diminishing, and the Japanese tourists started to come back but not in great numbers. The locals were his main customer pipeline, and many of them in the service industries were moving to the mainland. Shaloha Gems was cutting into his business sales significantly. He made a price comparison on similar quality diamonds and gems and realized that he could not compete with Shaloha, certainly not in the high-end space. He decided to set up a meeting with Abe Goldstein to discuss their business relationship and make him an offer he could not refuse.

Adam had already returned from New York after his dalliance with Shoshanna. Abe noticed his uncharacteristic daydreaming and giddy persona and realized that his pal was lovestruck.

"Bombastic, snap out of it. Your mind is 10,000 miles away in South Africa. I got a call from none other than

Kenji Ono of Ono diamonds and engagement rings. He wants to have coffee."

Adam scowled. "That momser (bastard) has some chutzpah after he pulled that move on you. Tell him to take a hike."

"Adam, we don't know that he did it. I want to see him face to face to see if I can read this guy. And more importantly, I want to know what this SOB wants."

Kenji left a message indicating that he would like to meet to discuss some business ideas that both companies would find beneficial. Kenji suggested that they meet at his offices in a high-rise building on restaurant row.

But Adam told Abe it would be best to meet in a public place and to somehow record the conversation in the event that Mr. Ono made a direct or implied threat. Adam added that according to the law, the unauthorized recording of a conversation is illegal unless there is no expectation of privacy, such as in an outdoor restaurant.

Kenji Ono arrived at the outdoor bar and restaurant accompanied by a stout Japanese male wearing wrap-around sunglasses, a sports jacket, and a silk shirt buttoned up to the top button. Abe noticed that it was a particularly hot and muggy day and wearing that sport jacket and shirt was out of place and must have been uncomfortable.

"Gentlemen, this is my business associate, Taka-San from Japan. He does not speak much English, so I will translate for him."

Abe began the conversation while Adam positioned the briefcase with the pinhole camera so that it could record the video and audio of the conversation.

"Kenji Ono, I am surprised that you wanted to speak to us," Abe began. "I can't imagine what you wanted to talk about. You brought your business associate Taka-san from Japan. What an honor."

Adam had previously instructed Abe to verify the identity of players so that there would be no mistake if the video recording was ever used as evidence.

"Mr. Goldstein, I see that you're spending lots of money on advertising on television. I hope it pays off for you."

"We are doing okay. Why do you mention it?"

"Well, Ono Diamonds relies on local business for our customer base, not so much for wealthy mainland haoles who want expensive designer island rings or pendants for their wives or girlfriends as a memento of their visit. Our company doesn't have the high-end inventory or jewelry design capability to go after that crowd. Your company does."

Kenji gave a tight smile. "We are just local boys trying to make a living, and Shaloha Gems is cutting into our bottom line. We have been in this community a long time and intend to be here a lot longer, longer than you will." He bared his teeth. "We won't be undercut by some New York Jewish haoles, do you understand?"

Adam decided to jump into the conversation and bait Kenji a little.

"Kenji and Mr. Takko," he said mildly, "that is what's called capitalism, free enterprise, the American Way. Do you have a problem with that? You said you wanted to discuss a business proposition that would help both businesses. We are all ears."

Taka-san leaned forward in his seat and glared at both Adam and Abe while Kenji Ono spoke.

"Goldstein, I strongly suggest that you concentrate on the high-end haole tourist market and leave the local wedding engagement ring business to us. Things will go a lot smoother for you if you do."

Adam replied, "Kenji, I detect a menacing tone in your voice. Are you threatening us?"

Kenji Ono stood up from the table, and Taka-san spilled his drink into Abe's lap, pretending the move was an accident. "Suimasen, Goldstein-san, sorry," he muttered.

Kenji Ono and taka-San abruptly left the table.

After they walked away, Abe turned to Adam. "Bombastic, do you think that little move was a not-so-subtle message by odd-job?"

"Absolutely. Notice odd-job was wearing a sports jacket and buttoned-up shirt on a muggy day?"

"Yes, I did notice that. Why?"

"Because full body tattoos are covered that way. Did you notice his left pinky, which he hid under the table the whole time?

"No, I did not. Why?"

"Because it wasn't there."

The following Sunday, at about five in the morning, a brick was thrown through the window of Shaloha Gems. The surveillance cameras caught a glimpse of a masked individual wearing a generic maintenance worker's uniform. No attempt at robbery was made. As a standard procedure, the valuables on display were put into the safe at the close of business.

The alarm company that maintained cameras in the store and the Royal Hawaiian mall security called Abe within twenty minutes of the vandalism. Abe and Adam rushed down to the mall, assessed the situation, and remained at the store until the Honolulu police arrived and filed a report. The CCTV video was reviewed from both the store and various locations in the mall and in the parking lot. It appeared that the masked vandal, dressed like a maintenance worker and wearing a baseball hat and gloves, walked in from the street carrying a gym bag that contained a brick. He appeared to pay attention to the surveillance cameras, turning his head away as he walked by them.

A glass company was called to begin repairs. In the meantime, a plywood barrier was set up to secure the premises.

The Honolulu FBI office was located on Enterprise St. in Kapolei. Adam called the duty agent and set up an appointment regarding a possible attempt at extortion involving organized crime in Hawaii.

Special Agent William "Billy Bob" Hansen greeted them in the lobby next to a photo of the current director of the FBI, who stared down with a smile of attentive idiocy.

Billy Bob was from Jackson, Mississippi. This was his third office after the Atlanta and Washington, DC HQ divisions. He took the transfer to Honolulu, a hard-to-fill office due to the cost of living and housing. He was promised a promotion to his next office as a payoff which he hoped would be to his home of Jackson. Honolulu was merely a way station for Billy Bob, who was doing his best not to break a sweat. Billy Bob's motto was "Big cases, big problems. Small cases, small problems. No cases, no problems."

"Gents," he greeted them with handshakes. "The duty agent mentioned that you believe that you were a victim of an attempted extortion. Is that correct?"

Abe answered first, describing the purchase of his business, the relationship with their competitor Kenji Ono, the meeting at the restaurant with Ono and a Japanese thug, Taka-San, and the recent vandalism at their store.

"Agent Hansen, my partner Adam videotaped the

meeting. Some of the footage didn't turn out so well, but the audio can be understood clearly. His implied threat at the end of the meeting and the not-so-subtle spilling of the drink on me was a message, and now the incident at our store at the Royal Hawaiian shopping center, what can we do? Obviously, he is attempting to intimidate us out of business."

The agent gave him a regretful look. "Mr. Goldstein, I understand your concern, but you must realize that we have no evidence that we can use to charge anyone or even enough information to interview him. His statement to you was implied and not a direct threat. Obviously, we won't be able to identify the brick thrower or connect him to Ono."

Abe and Adam frowned.

"But of course, we'll still check it out," Hansen added vaguely, steering them down a hallway. "Can you look at some photos of suspected Japanese organized crime figures that have traveled to Hawaii? The Japanese national police stay in touch with us regarding their movements to the states."

Abe and Adam viewed a digital screen with photos of various Japanese thugs and identified Taka-San in one of the photographs. Hideki Taka was a suspected member of the Yamaguchi-gumi, the largest of the yakuza gangs.

"Mr. Goldstein and Mr. Bushkin, we will do some research on Mr. Taka to see if he is here illegally. We will let you know if there is any judicial action. In the meantime, secure your premises. Unfortunately, there is nothing more that we can do at this point—"

Adam interrupted, "Agent Hansen, so I guess we'll have to wait until one of us is killed for you to open a case?"

Agent Hansen thought to himself that he had to stroke these obnoxious New Yorkers, not offend them, since they were the types that would file a complaint. He just wanted to write this up in time to get on the road before he got stuck in traffic on his hour-plus drive to his home in Hawaii Kai.

"We will stay in touch, don't worry," he said with a reassuring smile. "We are on it, Mr. Goldstein."

Adam and Abe left the office and drove to a local Starbucks to talk.

"Abe, you heard Billy Bob," Adam said dryly. "He's on it. Nothing to worry about."

"Adam, I don't get that warm and fuzzy sense of security after speaking to Agent Billy Bob. What was your take?"

He blew on his coffee. "I didn't expect much. My friends in the NYPD Shomrim Jewish law enforcement association used to say FBI stood for 'famous but incompetent.' As long as we documented the threat and the vandalism, we have set a timeline." He sighed. "I'll email agent Billy Bob and go over what was discussed today so that it's on record."

Abe and Adam next set up a meeting with Chikara Arakaki, who'd heard about the vandalism incident but didn't know about the previous meeting with Ono and his bodyguard.

Chikara met Abe and Adam at the Shaloha Gems store in Abe's office and shut the door for privacy. The glass company was working on reinstalling reinforced shatterproof glass that would spiderweb on impact but not break.

Abe told Chikara about the threatening meeting with Ono prior to the brick-throwing incident.

"This is disturbing," Chikara said, his brow furrowing.

"In all the years we were in business, this kind of thing never happened to us. Maybe it's because you are outsiders, and Ono knew that if we had to, we could push back at him. He doesn't think that you can, so he's seeing whether he can scare you."

"Chikara, any suggestions for us?" Abe asked. "What would you do? Would you call HPD instead of the FBI?"

"Well, HPD would do nothing," Chikara replied gravely. "They give discounts to HPD for their engagement rings, inflated prices, giving them a 20 percent discount makes them think they got a great deal, so the cops look out for them."

Abe chimed in, "It's like the New York cops getting free donuts and coffee to keep an eye on the doughnut shop."

Chikara simply said, "I would send in the stonemasons to have a discussion with them."

Abe and Adam simultaneously echoed, "Stonemasons?"

A terse nod. "Yes, I will introduce you to the stonemasons at the right time."

The following week, a representative of Oshiro's wedding company called Abe and advised that they would not be sending their Japanese tour groups to his gem store when the Japanese tourists returned to Hawaii since they got an offer from another company, and that they were now under contract and could not go to Shaloha.

Abe said, "Let me guess, you are working with Ono Diamonds. What are they paying you? I'll pay you more money."

Oshiro softly said, "It's not the money, Abe-San. You don't understand. They are *bōryokudan*." Violent groups.

Adam and Abe went to the Chabad house for Friday

night Shabbat services and the Shalom Café for the after-service dinner. Gilad was seated at another table and waved hello, "Shabbat shalom."

Abe walked over to the table where Gilad was seated with some other Israelis.

"Shabbat shalom, Gilad, if the offer is still good, Adam and I would like to join you for dinner one night soon."

"How about this Sunday evening at my condo at Nauru Towers, apartment 14J, at 6:00 p.m.? My wife makes an excellent brisket of beef with Israeli salad and home-made hummus, delicious!"

"We will be there. Is there anything we can bring? Wine, schnapps?"

Gilad smiled. "Just bring an appetite."

Nauru Tower was a beautiful high-rise condo over-looking Ala Moana Park with sweeping views of the Pacific Ocean. Abe and Adam looked out at the beautiful sunset as they sat down for after-dinner drinks. Gilad asked if either of them smoked cigars, and both declined.

"Do you mind if I smoke one?"

Adam said, "Please do, no problem."

Abe and Adam explained the situation and asked Gilad for some ideas regarding how to respond.

The Israeli lit a cigar, blowing a stream of fragrant smoke at the ceiling. "First, I would hire a private detective to do some homework on Mr. Kenji Ono and find out as much as possible about him, including who his customers are and his sources of inventory. Identify his computer system, where he banks, etc." He gestured with the stogie. "I have a good local private investigator who has a lot of connections, both kosher and non-kosher, if you get my drift. Let's see what he comes up with. After that, we have a number of avenues we can pursue."

Abe tensed. "No rough stuff, Gilad, I mean it."

"No rough stuff, of course. We just want to get Mr. Ono's attention."

"What's it going to cost us, if I may ask?" Adam inquired.

"Let's start with a $10,000 retainer."

KIMO ORNELLAS WALKED into the Ono Diamonds store on Kapi'olani Blvd. in Honolulu. A local salesgirl greeted him.

"Hey, sista, I'm looking for da kin necklace for my girl-friend. Not too expensive. You got anyting on sale?"

"Sir, we have some beautiful black coral necklaces, even Niihau shell necklaces."

"Sista, I'm a retired cop. I hear you guys give cops a break?"

"Can you show me identification?"

Kimo flashed an HPD badge. The salesgirl nodded.

"Ok, we offer a 20-percent HPD discount on all items across the board."

"Let me look at dat coral necklace. What is the price on dat?"

"One hundred fifty with the police discount."

"Do you have any others that you can show me, similar kin?"

"Yes, let's look at our inventory online to see what we have in stock and what we can order from our suppliers." She turned away. "Let me see what we have in the back room. I'll bring them all out for you to look at, give me a minute."

"Can I browse da necklaces on your laptop to see maybe der is someting dat catches my eyes?"

"Sure, Mr. Ornellas, I will be right back."

As soon as she left the room, Kimo inserted a flash drive into the laptop and pressed the enter button. He gave it a minute, then quickly withdrew it. The salesgirl came out, and Kimo exclaimed, "Hey, I was just skimming the different kine necklaces on your computer to see what other styles I might want to buy. Da black coral is beautiful, but I am not got dat kine of bread."

He chose one of the cheaper coral necklaces and told her that was the one he wanted.

When he tried to run his credit card through, it was declined.

"Mr. Ornellas, it seems that your card has been declined." Her face was politely neutral. "Do you want to call them?"

He scowled. "No, da buggas did dat to me. Maybe my ex screwed up my credit. What company do you use to process your cards?"

"Bank of Hawaii merchant services, why do you ask?"

"Because I heard dat bank has had problems with their merchant service, maybe dat's the problem." He flashed a smile and headed for the door. "Well, I'm going to straighten this out and come back later."

GILAD MADE a phone call to Israel, which was eleven hours plus a day later. Dudi Ashkenazi was a former Shin Bet white-hat hacker who retired and formed his own company handling interesting cases internationally.

"Dudi, ma shlom cha? How are you?"

"Beseder." *I'm doing well.*

"My guy inserted the flash drive into the ben zona's (son of a whore) laptop, so we are good to go."

KENJI ONO HAD lunch with Taka-San at a Japanese-owned sushi restaurant not too far from his storefront. They spoke entirely in Japanese.

"Taka-San, I think these New York gaijins got the message. If not, we might have to up the game and scare some of their salespeople. If they stop running commercials, that would be a good sign that they got the message. Send them a little present in the mail."

"Hai, wakarimasu, Ono-San." *Yes, I understand.*

"What is more important is the next deposit that you run through my store, we must keep it below $100,000 US a month until December, when we can up the deposits to about $1,000,000, explaining the cash as Christmas sales. You bring in the money from Las Vegas and LA, and I will adjust the inventory records to match the receipts. And when I open my store in Agana, Guam, we can double that easy."

Kenji Ono had been laundering drug money from the sales of shabu (ice) in LA and Las Vegas for the Yamaguchi-gumi for about five years. The diamond and gem business was a perfect venue for money laundering. Inventory could be fabricated, valuations could be enhanced, and bogus customers using credit cards from Japan provided by Taka could be utilized to give the appearance of a thriving business. With Shaloha Gems cutting into his legit business, it was harder to pull off and stay under the radar of the IRS.

At that moment, Ono's phone rang, and he was in a

heated conversation with his office.

"Taka-San, sumimasen (excuse me), I have to go to my office. Something is wrong."

The salesgirl at the store explained to Kenji Ono that the electricity had been turned off at the store, and when she called Hawaiian Electric, she was told that the auto-payment was not made. Also, the armored car that was due to pick up the receipts for the week never showed up and, when called, indicated that their records showed that the pick-up was canceled online, but she never canceled it.

Ono contacted Emiko the office manager, who denied any knowledge of what might have happened.

Ono started to panic, his palms sweating. Could the government be monitoring his computer and bank information? Did they suspect that he was laundering money for the yakuza?

GILAD MADE a late-night call on Signal, an encrypted phone service, to Dudi in Tel Aviv where it was morning.

"Dudi, boker tov," he said. *Good morning.*

Dudi replied, "erev tov." *Good evening.*

"So did you mess with our Japanese friend a little?"

"Yes, just a little. I think we got his attention. We canceled his electricity payment and his armored car pick-up. We also reduced the sales prices on his online inventory by 75 percent, so his online customers will be purchasing his jewelry below cost. Until he figures it out."

A pause. "He, of course, will know something is wrong and will probably hire a local IT guy who will attempt to determine if his system was compromised by some virus or malware. But our malware is unique. We call it Ninja-yid since we do our damage and lie dormant undetectable in his system until we decide to revisit it again.

"What is interesting about Ono Diamonds is since you mentioned that he was connected to the Yakuza, I noticed a pattern of cash flow and inventory consistent with money laundering perfected by our brethren around the world who sell ecstasy and move the cash receipts through Israeli-owned jewelry stores.

"There is an encrypted email system that is on his laptop separate from his business email that is written entirely in Japanese, specifically Hiragana and Katakana. I think that's where we will find out a lot about his operations."

"Dudi, can you break into that encryption program?"

"Break into it?" An amused chuckle drifted over the line. "Well, an Israeli company designed the program, and the Shin Bet regularly break into it monitoring our Arab friends, so I am sure we can."

"Toda raba." *Thank you very much.* "Stay in touch, Dudi."

ADAM AND ABE met Gilad at their favorite Starbucks at Ala Moana shopping center.

Abe started the conversation. "Gilad, tell me that I'm getting my money's worth and getting Ono's attention?"

"Abe, you are getting your money's worth — maybe not getting the ben zona's attention yet, but he must be concerned since my friend in Israel stopped his store's electricity payment to Hawaiian electric and canceled his armored car pick-up. He could have done more, but I just wanted to eff with him a little first and see what his reaction is."

"However, my Israeli friend did find something interesting — an encrypted email program on his computer, written in Japanese, as well as some patterns of monetary deposits inconsistent with the regular course of business and more consistent with illegal money laundering. At this stage, it's speculation until we can find a smoking gun which may be in the encrypted emails."

Abe nodded. "Gilad, our goal is to let this bastard know not to mess with us. Can we bring any information to the attention of the FBI if we find something?"

Gilad arched a thick black brow. "Abe, what we did intruding and accessing his computer is a federal crime, so if we brought it to their attention, your pal at the FBI would read you your rights and handcuff you. He would arrest all of us.

"No, there is a better way to handle this. Let's ramp this up a bit. I'm guessing he will seek some IT help to wipe the computer off any viruses, so now we will use the Ninja-yid program to hide our malware for the time being."

Adam chimed in. "Gilad, you are saying that no virus detection program will identify your malware?"

"Not unless it's got military-grade sensors, which I guarantee you they don't have."

Kenji Ono brought the laptop to an IT expert utilized by the law firm that handled his business. The computer expert ran a number of tests and checks for malware and came up with nothing.

Ono conferred with Josh Shapiro, one of the lawyers at the law firm that specialized in handling high-end white-collar criminal defense. The firm had a Japanese partner affiliated with a law firm in Japan that handled all of the yakuza prosecutions by the US Attorney's office in Honolulu.

Ono told Shapiro that "the glitch in the system shut down the Hawaiian electric payment and canceled the armored car pick-up."

Shapiro told Ono that "the IT guy said that he could not find any viruses or evidence of malware in the system. He doesn't know what happened except that it might have been that the bank or Hawaiian electric companies' systems were compromised, and the glitch emanated from that."

Ono replied, "That doesn't explain the cancellation of the armored car pick-up. Something is going on. Could the FBI be screwing with my system in order to monitor my business activities?"

The lawyer considered it for a moment. "Possible, but highly unlikely. They would have had to get a search warrant sworn before a federal judge to monitor your computer unless they did it under a national security statute. I think it was possibly a breach at the electric company and a simultaneous screw-up by the armored car company."

Kenji Ono's headache only got worse when he was called by the office manager Emiko, who advised him that their online sales volume had picked up by 50 percent, but the revenues were down 90 percent.

"How can that happen?" he demanded.

"Well, it looks like someone inserted on our website that there was a massive price reduction on a weeklong sale that everything had to go for 75 percent off, and half our inventory went out a big sales volume, but we lost money."

He ground his teeth.

"Also, Oshiro's wedding company was scheduled to bring a vanload of tourists to the shop, and they never arrived," she said. "I called, and they said that we emailed them from our corporate website and canceled the visit."

His fists clenched. "Emiko, how could this happen? Could one of our employees have done this? Have we had problems with any of our salespeople?"

"No, not that I know of," she said, sounding bewildered.

"You do not let this information out," he snapped. "Our business partner Taka-San can never find out. Understand?"

"Hai, wakarimasu," the manager said quickly.

Ono was not sure if the FBI was messing with him or if the New York Jews from the Shaloha Diamond store were behind it. He made another call to the law firm, but they could not give him an answer.

DUDI TEXTED and then called Gilad on an encrypted Signal line. "Gilad, ma shlem cha?"

"Beseder, beseder." *Fine, fine.*

"You have news for me?"

"Very interesting news. We got into Mr. Ono's encrypted email system. It looks like he's doing business with an organized crime group in Japan, the Yamaguchi-gumi. We used some Japanese-language software to translate most of the emails. They're funneling drug money through Las Vegas and Los Angeles, transporting the cash via courier to Hawaii, running it through Ono's jewelry business.

"Ono is now starting to move larger amounts of money into high-end residential rehabilitation centers that he owns under a corporate front name in Honolulu and Maui. Each of those three rehabs is running through one million a month, minimum."

Gilad blinked in surprise. "Why rehabs, Dudi? Why is Ono using rehabs?"

"Well, high-end residential rehabilitation centers charge an average of $55,000 up to almost $100,000 a month per person. They are perfect vehicles for money laundering since they rely on some insurance, but a high percentage of payments are in cash for privacy. HIPPA laws prevent disclosure of the residents, so they can simply say that they have 80 to 100 percent of their twenty beds filled, but really have only two to five beds filled."

Gilad shook his head. "I had no idea."

"Oh yeah," Dudi said. "Residential rehabs offer detox, psych counseling, acupuncture, hypnotism sessions, gourmet food, massages, etc., very pricey stuff, and they, of course, exaggerate their costs to maximize their profits and minimize their taxes."

"Between the diamond business and the rehabs, Ono and his business partners are running through almost three million a month."

"Toda raba, Dudi." *Thank you very much.*

"I'll forward the bill to you via email to resend to your clients."

KIYOKO GOT a delivery of a chocolate cake at the Shaloha store the next day. It was from King's Bakery in Honolulu. The cake simply had the hiragana (Japanese script) letter shi written on it, which means the number four, with two chopsticks vertically embedded in the cake. She called Abe immediately, hands a bit unsteady, and described what she had just received.

"Abe, someone sent you a cake with the number four on it and a couple of chopsticks."

"Is that a problem?"

"Abe, yon, the number four, means death, as does two chopsticks inserted straight up in the cake! That is a threatening symbol in the Japanese culture, meaning death, usually done in a bowl of rice. Two of our salesgirls quit after we got that cake. Abe, I'm very worried. I called my father about this. He wants to talk to you."

Abe and Adam met with Gilad at Gilad's apartment. His wife Levana had pita, hummus, olive oil, and olives, along with Kona coffee for them.

"This is delicious, Levana. Thank you so much."

She smiled.

"Gil, your message said you had some news for us," Abe said grimly. "Well, I have some news for you. That the ben zona sent us a threat."

Gil turned to his wife. "Levana, dear, could you let us talk in private, please?"

She nodded and discreetly retreated to the kitchen. Abe described the cake.

"Yes, I understand that this is a direct threat," Gil said with a sigh. "These are bad people. I told you that I suspected that Ono was involved in money laundering. Well, the encrypted emails confirmed it. He is also moving money into residential rehab centers in Oahu and Maui to launder even more money. He is moving approximately three million a month through his business with his business partners."

The Israeli smiled like a cat with one paw pinning a mouse's tail. "Ono's well insulated, but I have some ideas on how we can ruin his day with both his business partners and the FBI."

ABE AND ADAM met with Chikara Arakaki at the Shaloha store the next morning.

"Abe, my daughter was very upset about the threat the store received the other day. She told me that some of our best and most experienced salesgirls quit after she received the cake. It has to be that bastard Ono." Chikara's face was pale with rage and worry. "What are you going to do about that threat, Abe? I don't want my daughter to be in any kind of danger."

Abe held his hands up. "We have some things we are doing behind the scenes that we are working on that should get their attention. Unfortunately, the FBI is worthless in this situation."

"Abe, I may have a solution. Remember I mentioned the stonemasons? I think now is the time for a visit."

"No rough stuff, Chikara. We can't be involved in that."

"Abe, he threatened my daughter. I cannot let that go without responding. I will just get their attention for now."

Abe held the older man's gaze. "Chikara, please give us some time to get his attention ourselves in our own way."

Kenji Ono got a call from First Hawaiian Bank the next week.

"Mr. Ono, there was an unusual transaction that we wanted to talk to you about," the manager said. "It appears that your business account made a large purchase of cryptocurrency out of a company based in the Philippines. The girl who handles your account was out sick, and a substitute bank officer was notified who okayed the transaction after she emailed your office manager and got the go-ahead. That did not look right to me, so I thought I would call you."

Kenji checked the transaction and saw that over $250,000 was forwarded to the One Coin company in Manila. He was frantically trying to come up with cash to replace the monies diverted from his account and was in the midst of making phone calls at his office when two Tongan brothers, Mahey and Sulikai, who owned a stonemason business, showed up at Ono Diamonds' door. They were wearing their traditional lava-lavas and weighed in at about 300 pounds apiece.

"Howsit, hear dat you are having some trouble lately. Dats too bad. Maybe we can help you."

"How can you help me?" Kenji stared at the men. "What do you want?"

"Nutting, just wanted to say *Shaloha*."

They gave Ono the hang-loose *shaka* sign as they walked out of the store.

Meanwhile, the organized crime section at the FBI headquarters in Washington DC had information from the Japanese national police, including a copy of translated emails from a company in Hawaii named Ono Diamonds describing the extent of the money laundering operation involving Ono Diamonds and a Japanese organized crime gang, the Yamaguchi-gumi.

When the Japanese national police representative contacted the FBI liaison agent in Tokyo and provided the information on the Yakusa money laundering operation by Ono diamonds, he advised that the information came from a reliable source, implying that a rival Yakuza group in Okinawa tipped them off. Special Agent Billy Bob Hansen was notified immediately, and that bit of info ruined his day. He was seen murmuring to himself, "Big cases, big problems."

Gilad met Abe and Adam at their condo carrying a bottle of schnapps. They sat on the lanai, nursing their drinks and watching the sunset.

"Abe, I do not think you will be bothered by Kenji Ono anymore. He has a lot more important problems to deal with than Shaloha Gems."

"Great. Can you give me a hint at what happened, so I know that I got my money's worth?" Abe asked with a crooked grin.

"Well, let's just say we got his attention — and by the way, he just made a significant donation to Friends of the IDF charity from a crypto account in Manila." Gil raised his schnapps in a toast. "Very nice of him."

CHAPTER 10
BATTLE OF THE
MOTHER-IN-LAWS

Adam had been in constant contact with Shoshanna since he met her at the bar mitzvah in upstate New York. Calling her every day on WhatsApp, dealing with a twelve-hour time difference, exactly on the other side of the world. She planned to attend Abe and Kiyoko's wedding set for mid-September after the high holy days.

Abe and Kiyoko spent lots of time together working at the office and going to the beaches, to the historical sites such as Iolani palace, the last remnants of the Hawaiian monarchy, famous surf spots on the North Shore of Oahu (since it was summer the wave action was small) and landmark businesses like Matsumoto's Shave Ice in Haleiwa town. Kiyoko tried to make Abe understand the island culture, laid-back, complacent, simple lifestyle, with an underlying Asian respect for "kupuna" seniors. Abe even got used to taking off his shoes when he entered a home.

One weekend, Abe, Adam, and Kiyoko went to the outrigger canoe races at the Kihei Lagoon, where Kiyoko was competing for the Outrigger Canoe Club in six-person outrigger canoes in the women's open division. She brought a cooler with drinks for the team members. It was a colorful spectacle with the teams wearing team shirts, Hawaiian music playing with food, and t-shirt booths. All levels of paddling teams were competing, from keikis (kids) all the way up to the super-kupuna (70 and over.)

The two-white skinned haoles wearing flowered yarmulkes and aloha shirts, socks with sandals, and Bermuda shorts, did not fit in the crowd of onlookers and paddlers, wearing shorts, flip flops, and t-shirts.

Adam joked, "Abe, we are not in Coney Island anymore. I didn't see Nathan's around here, no parachute jump, not even a knish cart." He tilted his head. "Hey, I just had an idea. Maybe we can do a side business. We can sell taro knishes at canoe races. We'll corner the market, call it King Kamehameha Knishes. Triple K is a great marketing symbol."

"Hawaiian Ku Klux Klan knishes," Abe replied without cracking a smile. "I think you are onto something, Bombastic. Work on it a little more."

The Outrigger Canoe Club was the most venerable club in Honolulu. Their paddling teams competed around the world with a tradition of either winning or placing in most of the races they entered.

Kiyoko was the "stroker" in the number one slot in the canoe, the position that usually goes to the fastest paddler who sets the pace for the team. The race was a total distance of a half mile, consisting of a sprint to a flag, a turnaround, and a sprint to the finish line. Her team placed second in the women's open division. The top three teams in each division got flower leis and medals at the awards presentation. A few onlookers recognized Abe from the Shaloha commercials and said hello.

Abe and Adam were handing out drinks to the paddlers when a muscled and heavily tattooed Polynesian paddler named Kalani took a drink from Abe.

"Howzit, Shaloha guy, I have seen you on television. You are paddling too?"

"No, not doing any paddling today. I would like to learn, maybe I could join your team?"

Kalani chuckled, like *you got to be kidding*, and walked away.

"Abe, you should have told him that you come from a long line of Jewish watermen, that you are related to Duke Kleinamoku."

"Very funny, Bombastic, but I don't think Kalani would have picked up on your Borscht Belt humor. More likely, Kiyoko would have picked me up in the emergency room."

Kiyoko and Abe began preparing for their wedding. The wedding was going to be held at the Four Seasons Resort on the Big Island of Hawaii. Invitations were sent out to Abe's relatives in New York and Israel, and the guest list reached over a hundred on Abe's side. However, Abe realized that many would decline the invitation and just send money.

Kiyoko's guest list was also over a hundred, with some of the guests coming all the way from Okinawa. The Okinawans and Japanese would simply give money as wedding gifts. Kiyoko was required to send gifts to all of the invitees. She chose to send tea sets.

Abe had the daunting task of hiring a kosher caterer and bringing in a klezmer band from the Fairfax area of Los Angeles.

Kiyoko's mother, Hatsuko, was still not happy about her daughter's impending marriage to Abe and inserted herself into the wedding preparations. There would not only be a Jewish band, she insisted, but an "Eisa" taiko drum troupe and sanshin (Okinawan banjo) players. She also wanted a non-kosher food table where their relatives would eat traditional Japanese dishes, and a station with a sushi chef. The wedding venue would be divided into two separate areas, one for the Okinawan/Japanese and the other for Abe's friends and family.

Shoshanna and her brother Mordechai arrived from South Africa a week before the wedding, and assisted Abe and Adam in the preparations. Adam was lovestruck and spent lots of time showing Shoshanna and her brother around the island, flying over to Maui to scout out a location near the Maui art center for a second Shaloha Gems location.

This store would cater to high-end designer jewelry for the international art crowd that maintains homes there. Mordechai was a high-end jewelry designer and enjoyed the art scene on Maui; they all visited numerous galleries on the Island, and he identified a location that would be perfect for a shop in proximity to the art center.

Kiyoko wanted Abe to have more interaction with her family, so she insisted that Abe accompany the family to the Obon festival at the Valley of the Temples memorial park in Kaneohe. Obon is a festival that honors a family's deceased ancestors, and takes place during the summer, according to the lunar calendar. That is the time of year that the ancestors' spirits come down from heaven, and it's the families' chance to honor them.

The Valley of the Temples was in a beautiful setting near Kaneohe, overlooked by the green Ko'olau mountain range. The Byodo-In temple was a beautiful Buddhist temple and a replica of the temple in Uji, Japan.

Abe asked Kiyoko if Adam and his girlfriend, Shoshanna, and her brother could accompany them to the festival.

Abe traveled with Kiyoko's family to the memorial park and visited the grave of Oba-Chun, their grandmother. They said some prayers and swept and cleaned their grandmother's gravesite and, at the end of the visit, left some lehua flowers and mangos, their grandmother's favorite flower and fruit.

Abe explained that when he visits the gravesites of his relatives, he left a stone on the headstone to show that someone had come there.

Kiyoko's family proceeded to the Bon Odori dance, where the entire family joined in a mass of dancers circling a yagura stage where singers and musicians banging taiko drums and playing the sanshin banjo set the pace for the dance. The dancers generally danced in unison, waving their arms and circling periodically. Kiyoko was dressed in a blue kimono and waved a golden fan.

At one point, Kiyoko stepped out and insisted that Abe join Kiyoko's family on the dance floor, giving Abe a traditional "Happi" coat and a headband. Abe reluctantly joined Kiyoko and tried to follow her graceful movements. Adam got a great laugh watching Abe wearing a yarmulke, a kamikaze headband and a Happi coat stumbling through the dance routine. Afterwards, Abe figured that he had made a big enough fool of himself for one evening and exited the dance floor, joining Adam, Shoshanna, and her brother, who were laughing themselves silly.

Adam couldn't help himself. "Hey, Abe, did you hear about the Japanese Jew? Every morning on December 7th, he attacks Pearl Schwartz."

After the dance was finished, Kiyoko's family moved to an area near a large pond in front of the temple, where many lanterns were hung to illuminate the area. Kiyoko explained the lanterns were there to guide the spirits. Family members chose paper lanterns, wrote the names of deceased ancestors on them, lit the candles in the lantern, and floated them in the pond while a Shinto priest chanted, which was a ritual called a Bon Matsuri. It was a stunning spectacle to watch the lanterns float into the night, guiding the spirits back to the ocean.

Abe lit two lanterns for his grandfather and grand-mother, who perished in the concentration camps. Sophie and Abraham Goldstein's names were written with a black marker pen and flickered out on the water, Abe wondering what they would think about their grandson participating in what they would consider a pagan ritual.

Kiyoko Arakaki was working with her mother, Hatsuko, in making half of the wedding arrangements, and it was apparent that Hatsuko was not thrilled about the whole event and the marriage in general. She was in charge of the Japanese/Okinawan side, working with a Japanese wedding planner at the Four Seasons Resort on the Big Island. Hatsuko hired a Japanese caterer that served traditional Japanese food, including tako (octopus) sushi and ika (squid) sushi — which were considered "treif" (unclean and non-kosher) by the Jews — and Kiyoko suggested that a kosher sushi chef be hired so that there would be no offense taken. The banquet tables would be separate, and the banquet bartender would be instructed to separate the kosher wines, beers, and liquors from the non-kosher ones.

"Kiyoko," her mother declared, "if the Jews are going to have a clarinet band with men wearing funny hats, we are going to have an Eisa taiko drum dance troupe and sanshin players so we can dance too."

Miriam Goldstein still had tsuris (aggravation) about funding her son's accountant's love life and made Moishe miserable listening to her kvetching (complaining). She was in contact with the Four Seasons wedding planner that specialized in Jewish wedding events. A klezmer band was contracted from the Fairfax district in Los Angeles, and a local kosher caterer was contracted for the food, with kosher wines ordered for the banquet bartender. Miriam insisted that her rabbi in NYC officiate at the ceremony, But since rabbi Shmuley handled Kiyoko's conversion and she had grown comfortable with him Abe made sure he would handle the ceremony. Miriam mentioned that it was traditionally the bride's family that would pay for the wedding. "Ma in Japan the groom's family traditionally pays for the wedding."

"We are not in Japan, Abie."

"We are halfway there, ma, so let's split the cost in half."

The wedding was scheduled for after the high holy days that ended in the middle of September when the weather started getting cold back east. Miriam and Abe worked on the guest list, which they realized was mostly perfunctory. Most of their family would be insulted if they were not invited, but also would have no intention of traveling 10,000 miles to go to a wedding. Many would not come because the marriage was mixed, and they would look upon it as a "shonda" (a shame for the family.) The good news was that they would be required to send a present of some value because Miriam and Moishe had given their families gifts for weddings and bar mitzvahs. Miriam, with Kiyoko's input set up a bridal registry.

Kiyoko told Abe that she had good news and bad news about her family's gifts.

"Abe, the good news is my family would not use the bridal registry. They would prefer to simply give us money that would hopefully defray some of the cost of the wedding."

He nodded, silently bracing himself.

"The bad news is that with every wedding invitation, we have to send a present. A nice tea set would probably be acceptable."

THE FIRST MEETING was set up with the wedding planner at the Four Seasons Resort in Kona. Abe and his mother, Miriam, and Kiyoko and her mother, Hatsuko, met each other for the first time in the lobby, and it was" dislike at first sight." Miriam was wearing garish gold earrings and jewelry that Queen Latifah would think was over the top.

Hatsuko maintained her inscrutable look, but Kiyoko could see a palpable disdain in her facial expressions and body language. The wedding planner for the hotel, Leilani Kealoha, was a large Hawaiian woman with a beautiful smile and a pleasant disposition. She had been a wedding planner for over twenty years. That pleasant disposition was about to be put to the test by the "battle of the mothers-in-law." It was the immovable object of Hatsuko Arakaki versus the irresistible force of Miriam Goldstein.

Abe and Miriam sat on one side of the table, with Kiyoko and her mother, Hatsuko, on the other.

After the introduction, Miriam took charge. "So Lay-Lani, you know that this is an Orthodox Jewish wedding.

Have you ever handled an Orthodox Jewish wedding before?"

The planner smiled politely. "Yes, I have Mrs. Goldstein. I have handled numerous Jewish weddings."

"I asked you if you had handled an Orthodox Jewish wedding."

She looked puzzled. "What's the difference?"

"We, of course, have a kosher caterer and a chuppah tent set up for the ceremony, and of course, we will have an Orthodox rabbi officiating, and a klezmer band from L.A., with many Orthodox guests."

Hatsuko interjected, "Leilani, we are also going to have a non-kosher section of the table set up for my side of the family, and we have a drum troupe and sanshin player that will perform as well."

Miriam chimed in, "Lay-Lani, of course you know we have to have separate dishes for the kosher and non-kosher foods, and the buffet tables have to be separate."

Hatsuko gave Kiyoko a glance that said everything.

"Miriam, you mean you can't even have the same sets of dishes and have to use a separate buffet table, which will greatly increase the cost of the function?" she demanded.

"Hattie, that is necessary to maintain the kashruth of the meal."

"Kash root? What are you talking about, Miriam?"

"Cleanliness and separation of the foods that are treif, non-kosher and kosher."

"Cleanliness?" Hatsuko's brows drew down and her voice rose. "What, do you think our food is *unclean*?"

At that point, Abe and Kiyoko jumped in and cut the discussion short.

"Leilani, we will work things out with you later. Thank you for your time."

As they both left the room, Miriam and Hatsuko glared at each other like two boxers at a boxing match weigh-in.

As Abe drove his mother back to the hotel, she said, "Abe, did you see that woman try to give me the evil eye? The "ayin *hora.*"

He suppressed a sigh. "Ma, she did not give you any kind of evil eye. She just thought that you insulted her. Kiyoko will explain it to her."

"That woman is an anti-Semite," Miriam announced tartly, "and my son is marrying her daughter!"

"Ma, how do you know she's an anti-Semite? She probably doesn't know any Jews. In Hawaii, there aren't enough Jews to hate." He glanced over. "Give her a chance to get to know you. *Then* she'll hate you."

ABE AND KIYOKO were kept busy working with the wedding planner Leilani. It was agreed to have two separate buffet tables and that the wedding venue would be set up to have two separate sections, one with the Japanese buffet table and the other with the kosher table. The rabbi would officiate the service under the traditional chuppah tent with a klezmer band starting, and a break for the taiko drum troupe to perform.

Later, Abe called his bride-to-be on the phone. "Kiyoko, maybe it wasn't such a good idea putting those two together. It was like Golda Meir meets Mrs. Arafat."

A few weeks later, Abe's guests started to arrive from back east, New York and New Jersey.

The Yeshiva boys, Orthodox Jewish students who attend a religious academy, arrived at Kailua Kona Airport after flying all night from JFK Airport. Shlomo and Yitzie looked at each other in amazement. In New York-accented English, Shlomo blurted out, "Yitzie, it looks like we are on the surface of the moon."

The Yeshiva troupe looked out of place at Kona Airport, wearing yarmulkes and tzitzi strings hanging from their waists. Their parents looked equally out of place, with the Orthodox women wearing head coverings and full-length dresses. The men were wearing black pants, tzitzi strings, and white shirts, looking equally uncomfortable. Heads turned at the airport where the average local's daily wardrobe consisted of a fish-designed T-shirt, shorts, and flip flops.

Abe was tasked to entertain his guests and set up events, especially for the younger guests. A Hawaiian luau show was arranged (minus the emu pig-cooking segment), a zip line excursion, as well as an evening snorkel off a boat with manta rays, which challenged the yeshiva students to put on the snorkels and masks ditching their yarmulkes.

Kiyoko's relatives and friends came in from Oahu and Maui, where her grandfather Masaru was born on a sugar plantation. Many Okinawans worked on the sugar planta-tions until the war, when many volunteered for the 100th infantry battalion and later the 442nd regimental combat teams. Other mainland Japanese were relocated to deten-tion centers.

Masaru volunteered for the 100th infantry battalion and later for the 442nd RCT at age eighteen, along with many of his high school friends who had remained on Maui and still worked in the sugarcane fields. Some even moved to Oahu to work in the Dole pineapple fields and cannery. These local boys were shipped out to Fort Dix, New Jersey, on the East Coast, and would later be sent to Europe, where they distinguished themselves as the most highly decorated US Army unit in the Second World War.

Kiyoko would occasionally visit her one-hundred-year-old grandfather at the assisted living center where Masaru stayed. He was confined to a wheelchair, but his mind was still very sharp. Kiyoko would wheel Masaru around the grounds of the facility, with her grandfather always wearing his 442nd "Go for Broke" baseball cap and a smile on his wrinkled, kind face.

"Oji (grandpa), I'm getting married to a wonderful man, we are getting married on the Big Island in Kona, and we are going to bring you there for the wedding," she said happily.

"Kiyoko, dats nice, he good man, local boy?"

"Oji, he's a good man but not a local boy. He is a Jewish man from New York who is in the diamond business."

His brows lifted in surprise, a gentle smile warming his face. "Kiyoko, you know a Jewish man helped me start in the diamond business here in Oahu when I came home from da war. He taught me everything about the business and sold me his business when he got sick, heart trouble. Jews are smart and educated, strong aina (family)."

"Oji, I know he is very kind, and I love him, but my mother is not happy about it. "

Masaru laid a gnarled hand over hers. "Kiyoko, dats okay, your mother is not marrying him. You are."

CHAPTER 11
MASARU ARAKAKI:
BEGINNINGS

Masaru Arakaki was born in Kahului, Maui in 1923, one of nine brothers and sisters on a sugar plantation living in corrugated huts owned by the sugar company. His father Nakoto was issei (a first-generation immigrant) from Okinawa.) Little "Masa" did not own shoes until he was in grammar school, and they were hand-me-downs from older brother Hideki. Masa attended Japanese school after regular classes while Oto-san, his father, worked in the cane fields, and his mother Oka-san worked in the lunch hall as a cook for the Japanese and Okinawan farm hands.

Masa would entertain himself by going for swims in the ocean with his friends, fishing in the river for Opu, a small black freshwater fish, and getting into mischief.

The Japanese worked under a "luna," a Portuguese field boss who would ride a horse in the field and treat his workers harshly, requiring them to pay him tribute by giving him fish, fruit, and presents on Sundays when they were off from work. One day, the luna whipped Masaru's father for loading a truck incorrectly. In response, his father pulled him off the horse and beat him up. His father was fired and was almost arrested. That incident forced Masaru's entire family to move to Oahu, where his father got a job at the Dole pineapple factory.

"Oto-san, what happened? Why we have to go to Honolulu?"

"Betta to be fired den be dishonored, Masaru. We do betta in Honolulu."

The job at the Dole factory was better than working on the sugar plantation in Maui. The pay was better and so were the living conditions. The haole (white) managers, owners of the pineapple company, drove around in big cars and lived in a big plantation house. The haole manager's sons were Masa's age and he got to know one of them, a boy named William, while fishing. Masa's parents discouraged him from befriending a haole boy since it was accepted that they were a higher class than the Japanese. The haoles had a clubhouse on a golf course and the Japanese kids used to sneak up to the windows and watch the haoles dance wearing fancy clothes.

Masaru and his brothers attended Japanese schools in Oahu and where the discipline was strict. Shushin, a moral education, was emphasized which was an obligation to family and respect for one's parents, elders, and ancestors. Shushin prioritized honesty, hard work, obedience, perseverance, stoicism, loyalty, and family honor. The young boys learned judo and kendo (a form of fencing). In a Japanese home the males ate first, and Masa remembers Oto-san at the head of the table saying "oi," which meant bring the sake. There were not a lot of displays of affection like hugging and kissing in an Okinawan Japanese household.

Masa would volunteer once a week at the Hongwanji

Mission Temple of Jodo Shinshu Buddhism where he helped the monks clean the temple. When someone was ill, Oka-san would come to the temple, light "foo sticks", plant them in the small sandbox in front of the buddha and say prayers to help them get better.

While he volunteered at the temple, he met a young Japanese Nisei girl (second generation) like himself who also volunteered to do office work for the for the Shinto priest. Katsue was a sweet young lady from a prominent Japanese family, who worked for a Jewish diamond and gem merchant in Honolulu. Since Masa was Okinawan, he was considered of inferior lineage to court Katsue, so they met secretly on weekends at the movie theatre in Chinatown where they would watch movies and eat popcorn. Eventually, Masa stole a kiss during a romantic scene in *Gone with the Wind*. Masa and Katsue could never be seen together at a restaurant, nor could Masa ever call on Katsue at her home. The class distinction was that wide between the local Okinawans and the Japanese.

Masa played baseball after school with his friends. On December 7th he was playing baseball at McKinley Field when at around 8:30 am the police came with sirens on and told them about the attack on Pearl Harbor. Masaru and his brothers saw airplanes overhead with the red sun insignia on the wings, heard explosions, and immediately ran home. Masaru's father and uncles were rounded up and questioned by the FBI in the days following the attack. Although he was only seventeen, he joined the Hawaii Territorial Guard (HTA), which later became the Hawaii National guard. Masaru was in the 298th infantry regiment made up of Japanese men from Oahu, the 299th were from Japanese from the outer islands.

The Japanese from the 298th and 299th infantry regiments were sent to Schofield Barracks for training to form the Hawaiian provisional infantry battalion which later became the 100th infantry battalion. The battalion was led by two haole officers, Lt. Col. Turner, and Major Lovell. Both were held in high esteem, with Lt. Col Turner becoming a father figure to the young soldiers and affectionately referred to as the "old man." Later, Lt. Col. Singles took over the battalion and stayed with the 100th until just before the war ended.

Later, in 1942, the 100th infantry battalion was shipped out on the USS Maui and arrived at the port of Oakland, California, where a troop train was waiting. For Masaru, this was his first train ride. During the day when the train passed through the towns, they were ordered to pull the shades down so as not to startle the local residents. Before Masaru shipped out, Oto-san sat down with him and explained that whatever happened he must not "haji" (disgrace) his family, that he must maintain his family honor. Even though they were barred from citizenship by the 1924 Oriental Exclusion Act, they owed their loyalty to the land of their adoption.

The 100th infantry battalion then headed to Camp McCoy in Wisconsin, where the 1,500 men of the 100th infantry unit guarded two prisoners of war who were captured from a Japanese navy two-man submarine at Waimanalo beach.

In April 1943, after a month at Camp McCoy, the unit was transferred to Camp Shelby in Mississippi. The accommodation at Shelby was stark: corrugated steel huts with a single wood stove for heating. Masaru was cold all the time and would wear two or three undershirts in the evenings. Camp Shelby was segregated with separate barracks for white and black soldiers.

The 100th infantry division was combined with Japanese from the mainland who the Hawaiians derisively called "Kotonks." The Kotonks in turn called the Hawaiians "Buddhaheads." There were disagreements, even resulting in fistfights between the mainland Japanese and Hawaiian Japanese. The Hawaiians were more informal, while the mainland Japanese were more competitive, and they would make fun of the Hawaiian Japanese "pidgin" English. The Hawaiian boys believed in "share and share alike" while the mainland Kotonks were more for themselves. Most of the noncommissioned officers such as sergeants and corporals were Kotonks, which was a source of a lot of friction. The white haole officers were tasked with bringing these two groups together and promoted some Hawaiians to corporals and sergeants. Masaru was promoted to corporal.

The adjustment to Camp Shelby was difficult in that the climate was different — muggier, hotter, or colder than they ever saw in Hawaii. The diet was different. The Hawaiian boys were used to eating rice seven days a week; at Shelby they ate rice about once a week. The Hawaiians were not used to eating cheese or tomatoes.

The change in attitudes came when the Hawaiian soldiers visited the internment camp in Rohwer, Arkansas. The haole officers selected certain noncoms that were influencers such as Corporal Masaru Arakaki to go to the camps. The internment camp at Rohwer, Arkansas was very large with row after row of barracks, barbed wire fences, and guard towers with guards and guns. Right then and there the attitudes toward the mainlanders started changing, with the Hawaiians realizing that many of the Kotonks had family interned at the camp. As soon as they got back to Camp Shelby their attitudes changed, the word went out like wildfire. Corporal Masa told his fellow Hawaiians about the internment camp. After that, they were all "blood brothers."

On February 1, 1943, the 442nd regimental combat team was formed. Except for the officers who were mainly Caucasian, it was composed entirely of Japanese Americans. The officers remarked that this group of Japanese American soldiers were the best troops that they had ever trained. They excelled in the simulated war games at Camp Shelby and eventually due to their excellent training record, the status of Japanese Americans was reversed. Once enemy aliens, they were now being actively recruited for the US military from the internment camps.

In September 1943, units from the 100th infantry battalion were shipped to Europe and joined General Mark Clark's Fifth Army in Italy in initially non-combat roles. Then after proving themselves, they were later given combat assignments in which they performed in an exemplary manner. That paved the way for the 442nd who had just completed their training at Camp Shelby to join the 100th in Salerno, Italy. They were hit hard by the Germans at Monte Cassino, an impenetrable fortress where many men were wounded. General Clark would use the 100th battalion as the point unit where the Germans were the strongest since he knew they could get the job done.

Corporal Masaru was wounded at Monte Cassino when he charged a machine gun nest with members of his platoon. He took them out with a grenade but caught a round in his arm. Luckily, it was a superficial wound, but it sent him back to a field hospital for a two-week stay. Corporal Masa was awarded the Purple Heart for his injury and a Bronze Star for his actions, and later he was promoted to sergeant after he returned to his unit.

Sergeant Masa stayed in touch with Katsue and wrote letters to her at least once a week or whenever he could. He would receive letters back from Katsue, and she advised him that she had told her parents about him. The fact that he won a Bronze Star for bravery probably affected her parents' decision to allow the relationship to continue.

In July 1944, the 100th battalion and 442nd RCT moved up the coast of Italy to Luciana for the control of Livorno, a seacoast town. Hill 140 was the high ground that the Germans fortified that obstructed the 442nd advance to Luciana. The Germans pounded the 442nd with artillery fire, using their dreaded 88mm Flak artillery. Sergeant Masa and his platoon were in a holding pattern for a month until the Germans retreated from the area.

The men of the 442nd were transported to Naples, where in September they boarded transport ships to Marseille, France. In Marseille, they boarded trucks and animal transport rail cars for a three-day trip to the Vosges mountains of France. There they joined the 36th division of the seventh army. The winter was approaching and the 442nd did not have winter wear with them. Sergeant Masa's pal, Sergeant Takara, complained that they were going to freeze their "okoles" (asses) off before they got to the Germans. The average soldier in the 442nd was only about 5'6" or 5'7" and 145-150 pounds, so the weight of a heavy overcoat would make it hard to maneuver. The weather was cold and rainy, making the 442nd troops miserable. The Germans were entrenched in their positions and since the region bordered Germany, the Germans were determined not to give an inch.

The Germans laid an extensive network of mines and booby traps and used a new, anti-personnel mine called a

"Bouncing Betty" that exploded in midair and peppered everything with shrapnel. The casualties mounted within the 442nd. Sergeant Ohama, a medic, attempted to help a wounded soldier holding a white flag, but the Germans shot at and injured him anyway. That action so infuriated the men in Sergeant Masa's platoon that he and his men retaliated with a "banzai" charge that was so spontaneous and so furious it took the Germans by surprise. The Germans were helplessly trapped in their foxholes and were all killed with close combat rifle fire. That hill became famous and was from then on known as "Banzai Hill."

On October 23, the 442nd reached the French town of Biffontaine, where they attempted to get a well-earned rest. Their commanding officer was notified that a battalion from Texas, the First Battalion, 141st regiment 36th division, had advanced too far and were trapped by the Germans, unable to fight their way out. General Dahlquist wanted them rescued at any cost and selected the 100th battalion and 442nd combat regiment team to do the job.

At one point the men were immobilized due to heavy enemy fire. General Dahlquist and his aide went to Colonel Pence, the commander of the 442nd, and ordered that his men "get off their asses and move."

The general's aide was killed by sniper fire almost immediately afterwards. The 442nd could no longer rely on artillery support, and the terrain prevented tanks from getting in. The men of the 442nd fixed bayonets in an all-out effort. Sergeant Masa was firing from his hip in a "go for broke" charge at the Germans. Four days later, they completed the rescue mission. The 211 men of the "lost battalion" greeted their rescuers with cheers and tears of relief. The casualty rate of the 442nd in the rescue attempt was four times the number of soldiers rescued.

In mid-March of 1945, General Mark Clark asked General Eisenhower for the return of the 442nd to his command in the Italian theater. The fifth army failed to break though the western end of the German "Gothic" line. The Gothic line was a string of over 2,000 dugouts and bunkers with mortars and gun nests cut into the Apennines chain of mountains along the Italian peninsula in an area called the Po Valley. The 442nd frequently worked with Italian partisans who had detailed knowledge of the terrain. As soon as the 442nd would liberate a town, the partisans would round up collaborators and line them up and execute them. The Germans finally surrendered on May 8, 1945. The 442nd was assigned to search, process, and house the German prisoners of war.

Members of the 442nd, including Sergeant Masa, accompanied the 522nd field artillery battalion into Germany. Sergeant Masa was riding on a M-35 reconnaissance vehicle when they reached the gates of Dachau concentration camp.

CHAPTER 12
KLEZMER VS TAIKO

The last-minute wedding preparations were made with Kiyoko and her mother and Abe and Miriam.

Abe and Kiyoko agreed to attempt to keep Miriam and Hatsuko as far apart as possible. Miriam worked with Leilani and Hatsuko with another Japanese wedding planner from the hotel, and the two wedding planners coordinated with each other.

The wedding venue was to be divided into the Okinawan/Japanese side and the Jewish side. Rabbi Shmuley, who worked with Kiyoko for many months on her conversion to Judaism, was officiating,

The beachfront site of the wedding at the Four Seasons was beautiful and was set up with the "chuppah" tent where the service would be conducted. Guests started to arrive. A violinist played while they seated themselves. The groom's party and best man, Adam, arranged themselves on one side of the chuppah, with Kiyoko's best friend from high school, Amie, the maid of honor, and bridesmaids on the other side of the tent.

The procession of the wedding party began with Abe, Miriam, and Moishe, arm in arm with consideration for Moishe, who was walking slowly with a cane down the aisle. The bride and her parents, Hatsuko and Chikara, followed up, and the couple faced each other under the chuppah.

Rabbi Shmuley officiated the ceremony, during which Kiyoko circled Abe the traditional seven times. The couple exchanged the sacred vows that have been made at Jewish weddings for three thousand years: As Abe put the ring on Kiyoko's finger, the rabbi said the vow in Hebrew, and Abe and Kiyoko repeated it together in English. "Behold thou art consecrated unto me with this ring according to the law of Moses and of Israel."

At the conclusion, the best man, who was Adam, placed a crystal glass in a napkin, which Abe dramatically stepped on to cheers of "Mazel Tov, Mazel Tov!"

"Ladies and gentlemen, I present to you Mr. and Mrs. Abe and Kiyoko Goldstein!"

Cameras clicked as the bride and groom walked down the aisle with Abe's family offering congratulations. Kiyoko's family smiled but remained stoic.

Miriam Goldstein had set up the klezmer band from Los Angeles, and the band leader Hymie Horowitz was the singer and master of ceremonies. The cake-cutting ceremony began with a sloppy slice eaten by Abe.

Hymie announced, "Abe and Kiyoko will have the first dance." The violin played, "Oh, how we danced on the night we were wed."

The klezmer band then picked up the pace and started playing faster with the yeshiva boys jumping out onto the dance floor, dancing together in circles, arm in arm. As the pace got faster, the dancers' enthusiasm peaked with one of the yeshiva boys jumping in the middle of the circle doing a version of the Russian "kazatske" from a squatted position kicking his legs to shouts from the audience.

The band struck up a version of "Hava Nagila," with all of the members of Abe's family and friends joining in, culminating with the chair dance where the bride and groom are lifted up on chairs, pushed up and down accompanied by shouts and music. At one point, a handkerchief was produced and held at each end by Abe and Kiyoko.

Hatsuko Arakaki and the family and friends were taken aback watching what they considered the "wild antics" of the Jews dancing. Hatsuko huddled with her Japanese wedding planner and Glenn Ige, the head of the Eisa Taiko drum dance troupe.

"Okay, the Jews made a big splash," she whispered. "Let's show 'em how the Uchunanchu (Okinawans) do it."

Glenn Ige gathered his elaborately dressed drummers together, holding their large red taiko drums, and began the rhythm and chant. A sanshin banjo accompanied the dancers. The drummers lifted their legs up simultaneously while beating the drum, while the band leader led the group in unison with whistles and chants.

"Ha, Ha eiya kasa," to double drumbeats, "Ku ami, kiya sasa, Ha, Ha, Ha," with drumbeats on each *Ha*. The drummers whistled, "Sup eiya kasa."

Miriam murmured that she thought that it was some kind of pagan ritual dance. Her girlfriend Sadie quipped, "Maybe this is a fertility dance, so you'll get a grandson out of it!"

Miriam, not to be outdone, huddled with Hymie, the band leader. "Okay, Hymie can you do a bottle dance with the yeshiva boys?"

"The meanest."

As soon as the dance floor was cleared, Hymie's klezmer band struck up the clarinets and cymbals while two yeshiva boys placed bottles on their heads, arm-in-arm with each other balancing the bottles as they danced to the clarinets. The other yeshiva boys joined them and kneeled with their arms on each other's shoulders moving in unison to the music. Abe's family and friends clapped wildly.

Not to be outdone, the Okinawan and Japanese guests were prompted by Hatsuko to come onto the dance floor and join in with the Taiko troupe in tune to the sanshin banjo, waving their arms freely in an Okinawan kachashi dance, gracefully moving to the drumbeat, occasionally spinning around, the men dancing with a closed fist, and the women with an open hand gesture.

Abe, Kiyoko, and the wedding party joined in the dance, and Adam and Shoshanna picked it up right away.

There was not much interaction between the Jewish and Okinawan sides during the course of the evening. Everyone was polite, but both sides kept their distance.

MOISHE GRABBED his cane and slowly headed toward the bathroom. As he crossed the dance floor and walked through the Okinawan and Japanese guests, he noticed an elderly man in a wheelchair not far from the restrooms. The man was wearing a 442nd regimental combat team baseball cap with a "Go for Broke" slogan on it.

"Excuse me, sir, but were you in the 442nd?" Moishe studied Masaru's face and felt it was somehow familiar.

Masaru responded, "Yes, yes, I was. We called

ourselves the Go for Broke Regiment. How do you know about dis? It was long ago, 1945."

Moishe's heart began to thump. "I know because your guys liberated Dachau, where I was kept by the Germans."

Then it all came back . . .

On April 25, 1945, Abraham Goldstein and his ten-year-old son Moishe began the trek from Lager Ten slave labor camp in Bavaria to Dachau, accompanied by SS guards with dogs that snarled and snapped at any stragglers. Shmuel's wife Sophie had been separated from them with the rest of the women and were never seen again.

Abraham, Moishe, and their fellow prisoners were little more than walking skeletons. The guards beat and kicked anyone who fell down. For the first time, Shmuel noticed that the guards seemed anxious as the ragged column hobbled along the road. Allied warplanes occasionally roared overhead.

The next morning, they resumed their trek, and by afternoon they filed down a red brick road and through a gatehouse with the same cynical motto seen at other camps, wrought in iron, the words "Arbeit Mach Frei." *Work sets you free.*

A wave of dread washed over Abraham, and although he tried not to show that to his young son, Dachau smelled of death. Shmuel and Moishe were herded along with other newcomers to the back of the camp, where they were told to undress for the shower room. A sense of terror ripped at Abraham's guts, and Moishe could sense the fear. Others who came from Auschwitz to Lager Ten had told them what the showers meant.

The prisoners were assembled in a line when an American plane buzzed the camp. The German officers and camp guards got frantic and began calling each other on the radios. They decided to ignore the prisoners and began to assemble for instructions from the camp commander. Two or three other US reconnaissance aircraft flew over the camp, and many of the German guards abandoned their positions and fled in military vehicles out of the open gate.

Abraham yelled to Moishe to make a run for it. Many of the prisoners were taking advantage of the guards' distraction and were attempting to escape. Shots rang out, and Moishe hit the dirt. His father fell on top of him, attempting to shield him. Blood oozed over Moishe's body as he lay still, playing dead, not knowing whether this would be the end.

On the same afternoon, Sergeant Masaru Arakaki, and other elements of the seventh army's 442nd infantry divisions riding in trucks, hauling their howitzers behind them, arrived at the village of Türkenfeld, fifteen miles southwest of Dachau and just two miles north of Lager Ten. German resistance had all but evaporated. Regiments of German soldiers were surrendering to American troops.

As the 442nd units closed in on Dachau, Sergeant Masa later recalled driving through the gates of the camp and being shocked at what he saw. Hundreds of living corpses lying on the ground or propped up against the walls, unable to rise. Sergeant Masa noticed a naked young boy, no more than ten or eleven years old, weighing about forty pounds, a human skeleton struggling to get up from underneath a dead body. Sergeant Masa went back to his jeep, got a blanket, picked up the boy, and brought him to an aid station that the US Army had set up. Moishe had never seen an Asian before, and he was not sure who they were.

Sergeant Masa talked to him in English. "Yes, we are Americans."

Moishe was in shock and could not speak. Sergeant Masa gave him some warm soup and asked him his name. "Wie heissen sie?"

"Ich heiße Moishe," Moishe weakly muttered in response.

"Essen chocolate?"

"Ja, ja, bitte. Danke."

Sergeant Masa got some army fatigues for the boy and made sure he was taken care of and transferred to the medical unit. Masa's unit bivouacked outside the camp for a few days while the cleaning and interrogation teams were operating in the camp. Sergeant Masa made sure Moishe was okay every day and, before leaving, gave Moishe some more chocolate bars that Moishe kept like they were bars of gold, allowing himself to nibble on them, savoring every bite.

"Auf wiedersehen, Sergeant Masa, danke!" he called out in farewell, when the sergeant's unit was pulled out.

Sergeant Masa replied, "Auf wiedersehen, Moishe," to the scrawny little boy with the cleft in his chin.

Now, so many decades later at the Four Seasons Resort in Hawaii, Moishe could hardly speak, he was so emotional.

"I remember that I was rescued by a kind Japanese American soldier," he managed. "Sergeant Masa carried me to the medical tent, fed me warm soup, and gave me chocolate bars, the most delicious chocolate I had ever tasted. I remembered when he left. I cried when he said *auf wiedersehen*, till we meet again."

Masaru gazed at him in wonder, hands trembling where they clutched the sides of his wheelchair. "Yes, I remember the skinny little boy that I helped had a cleft on his chin. Like you do." He drew a deep, unsteady breath.

"My name is Masaru or Masa for short, and I was a sergeant."

The tears flowed from both Moishe and Masaru, and they began hugging each other. A crowd of guests circled the two old men crying in each other's arms.

Very shortly, Hatsuko, Miriam, Chikara, Abe, and Kiyoko joined the group and heard the miraculous story.

Masaru, choking back tears, said, "This was meant to be that we would meet. This marriage was meant to be."

There wasn't a dry eye in the place as Miriam and Hatsuko hugged. At that moment, the klezmer band struck up a rendition of "Mayim, Mayim."

Miriam led Hatsuko onto the dance floor and held hands in a circle. Other Japanese Okinawan guests and Jewish guests joined in the circle dance, clapping hands, and kicking left and right.

Back at the table, as Adam, Shoshanna, and her brother joined Abe and Kiyoko, Adam stood up and proposed a champagne toast to the new couple, followed by shouts of "L'Chaim!"

The Japanese responded with a "Bonzai, Bonzai, Bonzai!" cheer three times.

Adam turned to Shoshanna, his eyes bright. "Well, I have a special drink for you, a blue Hawaiian drink made famous by Elvis Presley."

Mordechai handed Shoshanna the drink, and as she finished it, she saw something embedded in the cherry. She pulled out an engagement ring and started crying. Adam got down on one knee and proposed, and she accepted. Abe announced the engagement to the party to more shouts of "L'Chaim!"

As the guests gathered around Shoshanna and Adam, Gilad pulled Abe aside.

"Your friend Mr. Ono, unfortunately, was indicted by a federal grand jury yesterday for ten counts of money laundering and wire fraud." A sardonic shake of the head. "The FBI raided the Ono Diamonds location and his residence in Kahala and seized assets and bank accounts. It was a terrible thing. His pal Taka was also arrested."

Abe raised his brows. "How did that happen, Gilad? I thought the FBI agent we dealt with said nothing could be done about it?"

"Well, nothing could be done about the extortion attempt, but my friend in Israel called in a favor from his friend in the Japanese National Police, who magically discovered some incriminating evidence linking Mr. Ono with money laundering for the largest Japanese yakuza gang, the Yamaguchi-gumi. That information was provided to the FBI attaché in Tokyo, who was compelled to act on it, and here we are."

Adam proposed another toast. "Shaloha to Mr. Ono. It couldn't happen to a nicer guy. L'chaim!"

Abe and Kiyoko and Adam stood in amazement viewing this miraculous scene. Moishe and Masaru were hugging each other when Rabbi Shmuley joined them holding a bottle of schnapps. Moishe and Shmuley were soon heard shouting "L'chaim!" Masaru replying, "Kompai!"

Meanwhile, Miriam and Hatsuko started arguing about the name of Abe and Kiyoko's first child. "Hatsuko," Miriam said loudly, "the first-born baby has to be named after my grandfather Mendel, so the child's name has to begin with an M."

Hatsuko crossed her arms and replied, "So if it's a boy we name him after Oji, call him Masaru."

"Masaru Goldstein." Miriam threw her hands up. "Are you serious?"

Abe turned to Kiyoko with a wink. "Looks like our mothers aren't going to be picking out furniture together anytime soon."

At the edge of the dance floor, Adam was all over Shoshanna like a cheap suit. Abe sauntered up to the love-birds and clapped his friend on the shoulder. "Bombastic, you might want to come up for air once in a while."

Kiyoko giggled and squeezed Abe's arm. The couple then walked over to where Rabbi Shmuley, Moishe, and Masaru were huddled in deep conversation.

"Oji-chun," Kiyoko exclaimed, her lovely face aglow with happiness, "this is wonderful that you met Moishe after so many years, it is truly a miracle!"

"Kiyoko," her grandfather answered, "Okinawans have a phrase: *Okagesama de.* It means that God must be watching over us."

Rabbi Shmuley chimed in. "The Jews have a similar phrase in Hebrew. *Elohim shomer alai,* God is watching over me, or *hashgacha pratit,* which means it was divine providence."

As the guests danced the night away, Kiyoko and Abe wandered out to the veranda and embraced while they watched the green flash of a Hawaiian sunset over the blue Pacific, knowing that their marriage was meant to be.

ABOUT THE AUTHOR

Born and raised in New Jersey, Terry Chodosh earned his MS in criminology from Florida State University. Terry began his twenty-eight-year career with the United States Secret Service (USSS) in New York City and fulfilled assignments in the San Francisco, Los Angeles, and Honolulu field offices, as well as in President Gerald Ford's protective detail. While assigned to the Honolulu office, Terry traveled extensively in Asia, conducting complex financial crimes investigations and providing executive protection for US government officials, including the president and vice president of the United States.

After retirement, Terry wanted to tap into his humorous and creative side, which was often restrained throughout his career, so he began writing his novel *Shaloha Gems*.

Terry lives with his wife and son in Honolulu, Hawaii. He enjoys distance swimming in the ocean and outrigger canoe paddling, and he strives to stay one step ahead of skin cancer and tiger sharks.